KILLERS AND KIR ROYALE

KILLERS AND KIR ROYALE

JANE GORMAN

Blue Eagle Press

A drop of sweat ran down Anna's leg, tickling the back of her knee. She didn't shift, afraid to wipe it away. Any movement could draw a swift rebuke. She glanced at Sammy, crouched next to her. Sammy looked calm and cool. She always did, even in uncomfortable situations. And this was definitely uncomfortable.

Anna risked a movement, rising slightly to adjust her stance and wipe away the sweat. The redheaded boy in front of her turned and scowled, the heavy binoculars drooping in his small hands.

"Shhh," Eoin whispered crossly before returning his focus and his magnified gaze to the swampland in front of them.

Sammy put the back of her hand to her mouth to suppress a giggle and pushed Anna slightly. Anna rolled her eyes and grinned before following the line of Eoin's binoculars.

From where she sat, even without the aid of binoculars, the immense bird wading in the marsh looked magnificent. It stood knee-deep in the water, as comfortable as any king looking over its domain. Beautiful gray-blue feathers covered its broad chest and back, its neck rising as gracefully as a swan's to a small but proud head. A tuft of black feathers jutted, crown-like, out from the back of its head, and when it shifted, more tufts appeared across its chest. As they watched, the bird opened its wings, and Anna gasped at the sight.

What had been a large wading bird became a magnificent beast, its wingspan easily six feet across. With its black-tipped wings open, the bird lowered its head and lifted out of the water, gliding gracefully over the surface before rising higher into the summer sky.

Eoin turned around again, that time his face glowing with delight. "Did you see that, Cousin Anna? Did you see that?"

He jumped up, and Anna took that as permission to stop squatting too. Glad to be able to get the blood flowing in her legs again, Anna gave Eoin a quick hug. "I saw it. It was incredible."

Eoin nodded eagerly, the sun glinting off his large, round glasses. He let the binoculars hang loose on the strap around his neck and pulled his tattered notebook out of his shorts pocket. "I can't wait to tell BethAnne about this." He led the trio off the small platform where they had been perched and back onto the main path, jotting notes as he walked.

Sammy grabbed Anna's hand, and they trotted after him. The sandy path led visitors to the Cape May Point State Park along a trail covering more than a mile of preserved nature, from marshlands to scrub pinelands to open pools of freshwater, before ending at the dunes that protected the sanctuary from the Atlantic Ocean. They'd chosen the longest trail option, just over a mile, and even though it was only midmorning, the August heat was already getting to Anna. She ran a hand across her brow as she glanced at Sammy, who smiled cheerfully back. While Anna felt like rivulets of sweat ran down her face, Sammy simply glistened. Of course. That's what Sammy did.

Eoin had paused on the path ahead of them, his heavy binoculars focused up into a tree a few yards away.

Anna padded silently over and leaned down to whisper in his ear. "What have you spotted this time?"

Eoin turned to pass the binoculars to her, pointing up as a grin split his face. "It's an eastern kingbird. Look! It's early in the year to see one."

Anna leaned closer to the boy so she could look through the binoculars, which were still on a strap around his neck. "Ooh, beautiful." She took a moment to absorb what she saw then passed the binoculars back to her young cousin.

"I suppose he knows everything there is to know about every bird here by now, doesn't he?" Sammy asked as Anna walked back to her.

"Probably. And anything he doesn't yet know, he's writing in his notebook, and he'll look it up as soon as we get to the library." She turned back to admire her cousin. "Isn't it amazing? I hadn't even met him four months ago, and now I can't imagine what it will be like when he leaves at the end of the month."

"Don't even think about that." Sammy draped an arm over Anna's shoulders as she frowned. "I don't want him to leave either."

Finished with his eastern kingbird, Eoin kept moving forward, leading the way as they came out of the trees and into the open space surrounding a large freshwater pond that bordered the dunes. The trail turned into a sandy bridge here, and a solitary figure stood looking out at the swans gathered in the water.

Anna's first thought was to keep a respectful distance

from the man, who seemed to be absorbed in his nature viewing, but Eoin had a different idea. With a friendly chirp, he let his binoculars bounce against his scrawny chest as he skipped over to the person. Anna's moment of concern passed quickly as she got closer and recognized Minister Woodley.

"Eoin." Minister Woodley smiled as he greeted the boy, pronouncing the Irish name perfectly. He wrapped an arm around Eoin, who smiled broadly back at him. "Anna, Sammy, how nice to see you all. I'm glad you're able to get out and enjoy this beautiful day."

"Me too," Sammy said warmly. "I'm always nervous about leaving the bakery, but I guess I need to get out of there sometimes, and this day was too gorgeous to skip."

"You do need to take breaks." Anna nodded her agreement.

Sammy ran the Wild West Bakery in Wildwood, a beach town just up the shore from Cape May. Anna had no doubt it was the best bakery around, and she knew that was because of Sammy's diligent attention to every detail in her baking and her customer care. But she also knew that Sammy couldn't keep going at the rate she'd needed to when first opening the business on her own. Since she'd become more firmly established, she needed to take time off sometimes. And that was where best friends came in handy.

"Just like me. I can't spend all my time cooking, cleaning, and taking care of guests at the B and B."

"You ladies have solid heads on those shoulders." Minister Woodley nodded gravely. His smile from a moment before vanished. "Life is too short... too short." He shook his head and looked back out at the swans.

It wasn't hard to pick up on the grief in Minister Woodley's voice. Eoin took his hand and silently joined him in staring out at the birds.

"Minister Woodley, can I do anything?" Anna asked.

She glanced at Sammy, who shrugged and stepped closer to add her support.

"Are you concerned about the police hunt?"

"Ah, that." Minister Woodley chuckled softly under his breath as he shook his head. "What a world we live in. Imagine, police tracking a killer to our little part of New Jersey."

Anna felt a shiver run down her spine as she thought about the ongoing police search. A man had shot and killed two people in Trenton yesterday, and while the state capital was more than two hours north of Cape May, the police had traced the shooter as far as Wildwood, and the search was ongoing. She hated to think that killings like that could ever come to their peaceful town. Well, peaceful except for the occasional local murder, that was.

"No, no, that wasn't what I was thinking about, as tragic as that is. I just... oh, I don't know." He looked up at the sky. "I like to come out here when things get hard. Seeing the nature that God created, that He gave to us. It helps me accept how small we are, that we are just one part of His greater plan."

Anna frowned. "I'm sorry you're feeling down. Did something else happen?"

Minister Woodley nodded and inhaled deeply. "That poor family. The Longhursts."

"Longhurst?" Anna wrinkled her brow. "I don't recognize the name. Do they live in Cape May?"

Minister Woodley shook his head. "Stone Harbor." He named a town about a thirty-minute drive up the coast. "But they're here often. I got to know James through his work in town. He spends a lot of time meeting with store owners, joining local festivals, that sort of thing. Oh—" Minister Woodley caught himself. "I mean, he spent."

"Did something happen to him?" Sammy whispered the question. Anna wasn't sure why, but the whisper seemed appropriate.

Minister Woodley looked around then whispered back. "He was found dead, you see. Yesterday. At the White Pine Winery."

"Angela's winery?" Anna asked, shocked, then put a hand over her mouth when she realized how loud her voice had sounded. "That's horrible. How did he die?"

Minister Woodley shrugged. "It was tragic, a truly tragic accident. Fumes, they say." He shook his head. "But of course, everything happens for a reason, doesn't it?"

Anna bit her lip. She suspected that many things happened for specific reasons but not the kind Minister Woodley meant. Fortunately, if it was an accident, James's death wouldn't pull her into another investigation. One glance at Sammy, however, told her that Sammy wasn't so sure.

They offered their condolences to Minister Woodley, hoping his outdoor meditation would help soften the pain in his soul at the loss of human life, and followed Eoin up the dune then out onto the open beach. The wind was calm, waves barely breaking out over the ocean.

"Another death in Cape May." Sammy looked sideways at Anna.

Anna shrugged. "People die. It happens. You heard Minister Woodley. This was a tragic accident—terrible but an accident."

"Hmm. We'll see." Sammy ran ahead through the sand to catch up with Eoin as he chased the gulls and sandpipers running along the beach. Anna followed as they made their way along the water and back to Sammy's car.

❧ 2 ❧

Sammy turned her eyes from the road to glance at Anna. "What's that look for?"

Anna realized she'd been staring at Luke's house as they passed it, just visible across the patchy field that separated it from the road. "Look?"

"Mm-hmm. Was that Luke's house we just passed?"

Anna nodded, trying and failing not to think about the hunky handyman who had helped her get her B and B back into working condition after she'd inherited it from her great-aunt Louise—more than working condition, really. He was not only gorgeous but also a talented woodworker, painter, even interior designer.

"And are you still refusing to admit that he's attractive and you want to go out with him?" Sammy interrupted her thoughts.

"Go out with Luke? Where are we going?" Eoin's high-pitched voice piped up from the back seat.

"We're not, at least not right now. It's just us." Anna glanced over to make sure the boy was still safely buckled into his seat. "But how about we stop for some ice cream?"

"Yes please!"

"I'm up for that," Sammy agreed, turning on her signal to indicate a turn off the main road. "But I still want to know why you're hemming and hawing about Luke."

"I don't know." Anna shook her head. "He's asked me out a few times now. But... it's complicated."

"It doesn't seem complicated to me." Sammy slid the car into a spot in front of the ice cream parlor.

Anna shrugged. "We get along fine when he's working on the house. But I have no idea if we're compatible in... well, you know, in a different situation."

"Right. And that's why you go out on a date. To find out." Sammy gave her a look, a look she'd been giving Anna all of their lives whenever Anna said something stupid.

Anna laughed. "Okay, fine. But I'd have to stop hiring him to work on the house—I couldn't hire my boyfriend, could I?"

"First of all," Sammy said over the top of the car as they piled out, "yes, you could. And second of all, he's done with all the refurbishing, isn't he?"

"True." Anna smiled down at Eoin and took his hand. "What do you think?"

"I think I want mint chocolate chip." Eoin licked his lips. "Two scoops."

Anna was still laughing as they stepped into the store. Cafe tables dotted the front half of the shop, lining the windows and filling the space between the door and the counter. Eoin made a beeline for the counter, where he walked along the front of the refrigerated display case, his nose practically stuck to the glass, his eyes wide behind his round glasses as he took in the plethora of ice cream options.

As Anna passed between the tables, she thought she heard someone whisper her name. She turned to look, and three neighbors smiled up at her innocently. She nodded a greeting and kept moving. A few tables in, she heard a distinct change in tone as she passed.

She leaned in closer to whisper in Sammy's ear. "Do you hear that?"

"Hear what?" Sammy tore her eyes from the ice cream display, which she had been eyeing as eagerly as Eoin.

"I think people are talking about me."

Sammy glanced around the room, waving at a few people she knew, then back at Anna. "Nah, you're imagining it. Why would people be talking about you? Wait—" She grabbed Anna's shoulder and spun her around. "Okay, just checking. Nothing's hanging off your back or stuck to your shoes."

Anna laughed out loud. "Okay, I get it. I'm being strange."

The trio ordered their ice creams then found an empty table at the edge of the room. Eoin was in the middle of a detailed explanation of how a great blue heron hunted for fish when a cough from a neighboring table caught Anna's attention.

She turned to see Sara, a woman she recognized from town, staring at her. "Sara, hi. How are you?"

"Fine, fine." Sara's head bobbed up and down quickly. "I was just... we were just..." She waved vaguely at the woman across the table, who Anna recognized but couldn't name.

"Yes?"

"Oh, well. You know. Murder." She grinned wickedly and pretended to shudder. "I suppose you'll be involved."

"Involved? Murder? Me?" She lowered her brows in confusion and looked over at Sammy, who simply shrugged and took another big spoonful of ice cream. "Why would I possibly get involved in hunting down a killer from Trenton?"

"Oh no, dear, not that. The murder at White Pine Winery," Sara explained.

"The death at the winery, Anna," another neighbor chimed in from across the room.

Looking around, Anna realized all eyes in the shop were on her.

"The death in the winery," Anna repeated slowly.

"James Longhurst." A patron nodded.

"From Stone Harbor," another added.

"Very mysterious." Sara finished the thought that apparently everyone in the ice cream parlor shared—everyone except Anna.

"We heard about that," Anna said carefully. "Minister Woodley told us earlier this morning. Terrible news, a tragic accident."

"Mm-hmm." Sara puckered her lips as she nodded.

"Maybe." Her friend raised one eyebrow.

"Oh dear." Anna put her ice cream cup down on the table and turned to face the room. "Okay, spill. What are you all thinking?"

"Well." Sara glanced around the room and received some encouraging nods. "I suppose you'll be investigating again, won't you?"

"Absolutely not." Anna spoke loudly so everyone in the room could hear. "I am so sorry to hear about this tragedy, but it has nothing to do with me. I'm not an investigator. I just run a B and B." She nodded with finality, gave a friendly wave to Sara, turned her back on the room, and picked up her ice cream.

After a second or two, the sound of chatter once again filled the shop, and Anna let out her breath.

"Wow. Tough crowd."

"So, will you?" Sammy asked around a mouthful of ice cream.

"Will I what?"

"Will you investigate?"

Eoin's eyes lit up at the question. "Another investigation?"

Anna glared at Sammy "No. And no," she added as she turned her glare on Eoin. "Why would I get involved?"

Eoin shrank back into his chair, so Anna made a funny face to get him to laugh again. Ice cream squirted out the side of his mouth and ran down his chin.

Sammy shrugged as she grabbed a napkin to wipe off Eoin. "You're getting pretty good at it."

"I only got involved in those previous cases because I had to. Why would I be involved in this?"

"What if Angela asks you?" Sammy asked. "It's her winery, and you've gotten to know her through your work with the small business association."

"Well, yeah, we're becoming friends. I don't know her so well."

"So?" Sammy prodded her. "This can't be good for her business, right? Someone dying in her winery? And maybe it wasn't really an accident." Sammy's eyes grew almost as big as Eoin's.

"I have no idea what you're talking about." Anna shook her head. "Yes, we're friends. Yes, a death in her winery can't be good for business. But that doesn't mean she's going to come knocking on my door and ask me to get involved in something that has nothing to do with me."

"Right. Got it. Well, better eat up," Sammy said.

"What's the rush?"

Sammy grinned. "We need to get back to Climbing Rose Cottage for when Angela comes knocking on your door."

❧   3   ☙

Sounds of water splashing onto the floor of the mudroom, accompanied by Eoin's high-pitched giggle, reassured Anna that Luke was keeping a close eye on the boy. A blur of black fur let her know that Tough Cookie had given up trying to stay dry in the mudroom. The small cat dashed out the open back door. Anna leaned over the table toward Sammy so her voice wouldn't carry from the kitchen to where the men were attempting to wash paintbrushes.

"My mom is coming down tomorrow." She glanced over to the open mudroom door one more time. "She wants to talk about Eoin and what's going on with him and his parents."

"Really?" Sammy's eyebrows shot up. "I didn't know anything was going on."

Anna shrugged as she shook her head. "She said she didn't want to talk about it over the phone, that it would be easier if she just came here, but I have to assume..." She leaned back in her chair and crossed her arms over her chest.

"She wants to question you about your life choices?" Sammy asked, finishing Anna's sentence.

Anna nodded. "I know she thinks it was a bad idea for me to reopen Great-Aunt Louise's B and B, and I know she wants me to go back to school."

Eoin trotted back into the kitchen, wiping his hands down the front of his already-wet shorts. "Back to school?" he echoed Anna's last words.

"How do you feel about that?" Sammy asked.

Anna slumped lower in her chair and looked up at the ceiling. "I just don't know. I admit, talking with Michael Chan and Tara White a couple of months ago got me thinking about my studies again."

"Not to mention talking with your ex," Sammy muttered.

Anna rolled her eyes but smiled as she did so. "No, not talking with the man who pretended to care about me while stealing my research and publishing it under his name. Of course not. But I can't make my decision just based on him."

"Definitely not," Sammy agreed as she pulled out a chair for Eoin to climb up on.

"I got a call from one of my former advisors—a non-lying, non-stealing, non-cheating advisor," Anna clarified as she saw the look in Sammy's eyes. "She was encouraging me to go back, said I was so close to finishing that it was a shame to stop. If I wait too long, all my research will be out-of-date, and I'll have to start all over again."

Anna chewed on her lip as she let her mind wander back to the time she spent in Puebla, Mexico. She'd spent months talking with local women about how they took care of their families, how they kept knowledge about traditional medicines alive. She closed her eyes and could almost feel the heat of the afternoon sun on her face, the citrusy, licorice-like scent of *hoja santa* and *epazote* as the women prepared their daily meals.

"Start what over again?" Luke spoke as he came into the room, breaking Anna out of her daydream. Only a few years older than Anna, Luke also ran his own business, the general contractor and handyman business he'd taken over when his father retired. His focus on his business never got in the way of his quick sense of humor—or the boyish grin that broke out whenever he thought of something amusing. His was a smile that made it to his pale-green eyes and showed off the strength of his square jaw, routinely covered in a five-o'clock shadow.

"Oh, just some questions about my old research," Anna responded airily, trying to ignore the usual thrill she felt upon seeing him. "Nothing serious."

"Nothing serious?" Sammy's voice rose, and she looked over at Luke. "I'd say making a decision about the rest of your life is pretty serious."

Anna gave Sammy a warning glance as she stood. "Eoin, you ready for lunch?"

Eoin nodded eagerly, and both women laughed. "Of course you are. You're always ready for food," Sammy pointed out.

Anna ran around the table to hug him. "I don't know what I'm going to do, but I can tell you all right now that I am truly happy here." She looked at her friends then down at Eoin, who looked back up at her, his eyes wide behind his round glasses. "With all of you," Anna added, giving Eoin a light punch on the arm.

Perhaps not as light as she'd intended, since Eoin toppled off his chair then scrambled to get up.

Luke helped the boy back into his seat. "I'm glad to hear that. I didn't realize you were considering leaving."

"I'm not," Anna said firmly, holding Luke's gaze. "I was

just saying that my mom was coming down tomorrow, and she always likes to ask me about my future, my plans, blah blah blah."

"Ah, got it." Luke nodded. "I have a mom too."

Anna's laugh was cut off by the doorbell. "Sammy, can you get started on some sandwiches?" she called as she ran out to get the door.

When she came back into the room with the visitor, Sammy was in the process of mixing up a bowl of chicken salad. She paused mid-stir to stare at their guest then burst into a laugh.

"Sorry, sorry." Sammy waved the spoon in the air. "It's not you. It's me."

Anna glared at her friend. "I think you all know Angela Nelson, from the small business association."

Luke raised a hand in a slight wave. "You own White Pine Winery, right?"

"Right." Angela looked at the floor. "I'm sure you've heard."

"We've heard." Sammy turned her face down toward the mixing bowl.

"We're so sorry." Anna invited Angela to take a seat. "This must be so hard for you. I do know what it's like to have someone die in my home, in my business."

Angela looked up at her hopefully. "That's right. You do. And even though you were upset, you helped the police figure out what happened."

Anna bit her lip, worrying that she knew where Angela was going with her comment. "Yeees... that's true. But it was a special situation, you understand. I mean, the poor man died at my breakfast table."

"And now someone has died at my winery. It's horrible." Angela looked down at her hands, clasped on the table in front of her. Her knuckles whitened as she tightened her grip, and Anna noticed a chip in one of her otherwise perfectly manicured nails. Knowing how much Angela valued being composed and tastefully dressed, Anna recognized the signs of distress.

Sammy ran over and put her hand over Angela's while leaning into a hug. "I'm so sorry. What can we do to help?"

Angela looked up again, tears in her eyes. "The police think it was an accident, but that could only have happened if I wasn't following proper safety procedures—if my tank room wasn't properly ventilated. If any of that were true, I'd be facing fines and penalties and maybe even have to shut down. Plus"—she shuddered—"it would mean I was responsible for James's death."

Sammy straightened and stared at Anna. "We can't let that stand. We have to help."

Anna looked around the room, at Sammy staring at her defiantly, Eoin looking at her eagerly, Angela with tears in her eyes, and Luke—well, Luke just looking really good.

She threw her hands in the air in surrender. "Tell me all about it."

❦   4   ❦

Angela sat at the kitchen table, staring down at her chicken salad sandwich.

"Sorry, it's not exactly fine cuisine." Sammy grimaced before biting into her own sandwich. "It's a meal fit for an eight-year-old."

Eoin nodded eagerly as he took another huge mouthful then followed that up with a handful of potato chips. "I mlove American mfood," he mumbled through his full mouth.

Anna leaned across the table to rest a hand on Angela's arm. "I'm so sorry this happened to you. It might make you feel better to talk about it."

Angela nodded, her silky brown hair sliding across her linen shirt as she moved. "Part of the problem was his oxygen meter." She picked up an apple from the bowl on the table and examined it. "It should have warned him." She took a bite of the apple and shook her head.

"Warned him about what?" Sammy also spoke through a full mouth.

"Apparently the air wasn't circulating the way it's

supposed to," Angela said between chews. "Not enough oxygen. He..." She put a hand over her mouth as she paused, and a tear slipped down her cheek.

"Right." Luke pushed off the wall where he had been leaning, perhaps not comfortable with Angela's tears. "I'll leave you to it, ladies. And gentleman," Luke added with a nod to Eoin. "I think I still have one or two final tweaks upstairs before I'm done."

Eoin nodded solemnly back, the spot of mayonnaise on his face notwithstanding.

"Was James a friend of yours?" Sammy asked softly.

Angela nodded. "A family friend. I'd known him for years, and now the police think I did this..."

"They think you killed him?" Sammy asked.

Angela stiffened, and she inhaled sharply, as if bracing herself against the idea. "Not intentionally, no. But he died of asphyxiation while stirring my wine. That means his oxygen meter must have been broken, and my ventilation system wasn't properly bringing in fresh air."

"That sounds like too much of a coincidence to me," Anna said. "I could see one of those things being broken, but both?"

Angela lowered her shoulders with a sad shake of her head and took a small bite of her sandwich, bits of chicken falling onto her plate.

"I do have some questions." Anna glanced at Eoin as he stuffed the last bite of his sandwich into his mouth and pulled out his notebook.

Angela nodded.

"First, tell me about James. You said he was a family friend?"

Angela looked surprised by the question but nodded. "Yes, he knows my parents. They were neighbors at one point. He's in the wine business as well, so I see him occasionally. He likes to stop by the winery whenever he's in Cape May."

"And that's what happened yesterday? He just stopped by?"

"No, yesterday I knew he was coming." Angela delicately dabbed at her face with a napkin and leaned back in her chair. "It was a little celebration, in fact. He'd just signed a new contract he'd been trying to get for years."

"Contract?" Sammy asked.

"He's—I mean, he *was* a wine importer. He'd travel to Europe, South America, wherever, visiting wineries and making arrangements to ship their wine over here. He'd just reached an agreement with a Chilean winery and wanted to celebrate."

"He was excited about getting Chilean wine, so he went to a New Jersey winery to celebrate?" Sammy raised an eyebrow. "Didn't his work kind of compete with your sales?"

Angela's lips twisted into a half smile, half frown, and she laughed softly under her breath. "Kind of, yeah. But I'm not big enough to see imports as competition, not yet anyway."

"So you were celebrating?" Anna prompted her.

"Right." Angela took a deep breath and leaned forward over the table, frowning. "We didn't have any visitors— Monday afternoons tend to be slow—so when James announced his big news, I popped open a bottle of sparkling wine and made us all Kir Royales, just to celebrate."

The scratch of Eoin's pencil filled the silence as Angela paused, shutting her eyes and taking another deep breath, working hard to control her emotions. Anna waited before asking any more questions, giving her time to compose herself.

Once Angela opened her eyes again, Anna asked, "So why was he alone?"

"He just wandered into the tank room. That's where my staff found him. He'd been stirring the wine, I guess, and was overcome."

"Overcome?" Sammy furrowed her brows. "By the wine?"

Anna shook her head. "By the fumes. The oxygen levels must have fallen too low, and if his oxygen meter wasn't working properly, he wouldn't have realized. He would've suddenly become dizzy and lost consciousness."

"So he drowned in a tank of wine," Sammy repeated slowly.

"Not drowned," Anna explained. "He died by asphyxiation. The air didn't have enough oxygen for him to breathe. Like I said, there are a lot of coincidences here. We're going to have to learn more. But I don't know…"

"What don't you know, Cousin Anna?" Eoin looked up from his book. "Can I help?"

Anna smiled at him gratefully. "Maybe you can. Who knows? It's just, this isn't my field. I don't know enough about wine making, let alone air ventilation systems. How can I help, really?"

Sammy shrugged. "With the help of your friends, like always. You can use what you know about gathering data and analyzing it, but you'll need to rely on friends who know the business."

"Hmm." Anna chewed on her lip, thinking, then turned to Angela. "I still don't understand why James was in the tank room stirring the wine on his own. In every winery I've visited, visitors aren't allowed into that room. They can only look into it through a doorway or window, and even then, they're with a guide."

"That's true," Angela replied. "But he wasn't just a visitor. He was a friend, and we were celebrating. To him, I'm sure it was a little present to himself. Like I said, he was always intrigued by the wine-making process, and he followed it closely. He knew which wines I was stirring and which to leave alone." She let out a little laugh. "It was something he always wanted to do, even when I asked him not to, and he always got what he wanted."

"I don't think he got what he wanted this time," Sammy said under her breath.

Anna glared at Sammy, but Angela simply nodded sadly and said, "Not this time, no."

Anna paused in the doorway of the guest room, looking in. Luke stood on a stepladder up against the wall, his gaze running over the top of the window casing. He grunted, shifted his weight, and looked again. Anna couldn't help but admire the way his shoulders and chest moved under his white T-shirt.

"Remind me why you don't want to go out with him?" she mumbled to herself. Loudly, she coughed dramatically, attracting Luke's attention. "There really isn't anything more to be done, is there?"

Luke grinned as he stepped down and walked across the room to her. Anna caught a whiff of his familiar scent, a combination of sawdust, sweat, and something sweet she couldn't identify.

"You're right about that." He nodded. "The house is complete. And it looks great, particularly this room. She would be proud."

Anna smiled sadly. Luke was right. Great-Aunt Louise would be proud. When Anna had inherited the B and B unexpectedly from her great-aunt Louise, it was in a state of disrepair. As Louise became older and unable to manage the house as a B and B, she had stopped inviting guests and simply left the upstairs rooms to themselves while she lived on the ground floor. Over the years, the rooms had slowly deteriorated, growing musty and tired.

In its prime, Climbing Rose Cottage had been a fashionable place to stay. Some even said it had hosted guests as famous as Oscar Wilde and Benjamin Harrison. Louise had kept up the elegance as long as she was able, and Anna was proud to have brought it back.

She was even prouder of this particular room. It was decorated with items from around the world—art, crafts, and other local products that Louise had picked up on her many travels. A Chinese tapestry hung on one wall. Polish lace covered the small tea table. Dutch candlesticks dotted the room. Anna's favorite piece, though, was the Queen Anne chair tucked up between the tea table and the fireplace, in front of a bookcase. She could just picture her great-aunt Louise comfortably settling in right there, a glass of dry sherry on the table, one of her favorite books in her hands. Anna had stocked the bookcase with volumes from around the house that ran the gamut from murder mysteries to scientific tomes and books on topics spanning from history to romance, anthropology to zoology. She agreed with Luke. Great-Aunt Louise would be proud of the room named after her. This was Louise's Room.

"I'll still be around. Don't worry. I'm not going anywhere." Luke pulled her into a light hug.

Anna wiped the tears from her eyes and let herself enjoy being held for a moment before stepping back.

"Right." Luke shoved his hands in his pockets and stepped back as well. "How about a little celebration for finishing the house. Dinner tonight? What do you say?"

Anna avoided his eyes as she walked around the room. "Did you hear what Angela said about this latest death?"

Luke laughed under his breath before he answered. He knew as well as she did that she was avoiding the invitation. "Only a bit, not much. What did she say?"

"The poor man, James, was overcome by fumes as he was stirring wine in one of the tanks. He would have been up on a ladder, leaning over it. He didn't even realize he wasn't getting enough oxygen. He would've suddenly become dizzy and just toppled over."

"Not getting enough oxygen?" Luke asked. "How did that happen?"

"To be honest"—Anna finally turned to look at him—"I know the chemistry but not the mechanics. When the wine is stirred, it produces carbon dioxide. That lowers the level of oxygen, and it can get dangerous. You hear stories about people getting sick, even dying, when that happens."

"That's crazy. If everyone knows it's dangerous, there must be a way to do it differently, to do it safely."

Anna nodded. "There is. It should never get to that point. The tank room has a ventilation system that circulates fresh air, plus James had an oxygen meter that should have warned him if the oxygen was getting low. So, apparently, both of those things failed to work properly."

Luke shook his head as he laughed. "Well, I know more about HVACs than I'd like to. I can tell you that. So if you have any questions about how the ventilation system is supposed to work, I'm your man. But, Anna." He walked over to her again and put both hands on her arms. "You didn't answer my question."

"I don't know. I'm so busy. Sammy and I are going to run over to White Pine Winery..." She looked up into his green eyes, standing out in his chiseled face. *What the heck is wrong with me?* "I'd love to go to dinner, Luke." She finally let herself smile. "Yes."

"All right." Luke tried unsuccessfully to hide his grin as he nodded. "All right." He looked around the room, shoving his hands into the pockets of his jeans. "And like I said, I'll always be around if you need anything else done at the house." He looked back at Anna, letting the grin cut across his face. "I'll head home now and be back at seven to pick you up." He looked her up and down one more time before leaving the room.

Anna let out her breath. She'd convinced herself that going out with Luke would be a bad idea. *But why?* He was attractive, clearly interested in her, and a good man. She shook her head at her thoughts. If nothing else, she could use the dinner to interrogate him about how the ventilation system and oxygen meter were supposed to work. Even if the date went badly, she could still get something useful out of it. But first, she needed to visit the scene of the crime.

✢   6   ✢

Two rows of tall pine trees marked the entrance to White Pine Winery, but the tree cover soon opened into a bright, open space. The gravel drive passed through a field of trimmed grass, the sides of the road lined with wine barrels. Instead of wine, the barrels held a profusion of colorful flowers that tumbled from the top and spilled onto the grass below.

Beyond the field, Anna could see row upon row of vines. The trim, organized plants came all the way up to the side of the winery, where a covered patio provided benches, tables, and chairs for guests to enjoy a bottle while taking in the peaceful atmosphere of the vines.

"Eoin would have liked this," Anna said with regret, thinking of Eoin's reluctance to stay at the library instead of coming to the winery with them. She hadn't thought a winery would be the best place for an eight-year-old. Looking around at the environment, though, she realized how wrong she'd been. She even saw a swing set tucked up against the edge of the patio.

"Don't worry." Sammy leaned over and patted Anna's

hand. "He'll be absorbed in a new book by now. You know he loves it there."

Anna laughed, picturing the way the boy's eyes lit up whenever he got to the library. "Too true. Isn't this place beautiful, Sammy?"

Sammy pulled into a parking spot in front of the main entrance. Gravel crunched under their feet as they passed between more flowering wine barrels that lined the path to the front door. A bird called in the distance.

Anna raised a hand to shield her eyes as she looked up. "That might be a hawk," she said. "But I suspect it's a turkey vulture."

"A vulture?" Sammy shuddered. "Well, that's not a good sign. Come on, let's get inside."

The front door opened into what looked like a small country store. To their right, a handful of low shelves displayed wine-related goods like picnic baskets designed to hold wine bottles, a variety of wine glasses, and corkscrews, and even decorative art made out of corks. A counter ran along the wall to their left, and Angela stood behind it, systematically zapping small wire brushes with a labeling machine as she unboxed them.

"Anna, Sammy, so glad you could come." She greeted them with a quick nod as she stowed the box under the counter.

Here, in the winery, Angela looked like a different person than she had earlier in Anna's kitchen. She projected confidence, moving with poise and grace that hinted at dance classes in her childhood. Her hair was twisted into a clip at the back of her head, and its silky strands glowed when they caught the light. The dark olive of the silk sleeveless shirt she wore over cotton trousers complemented her coloring perfectly. Her smile was welcoming and gracious, and Anna suspected that some expensive face creams might be involved in the absence of wrinkles on her face, even when she smiled. As Angela hid the box of wire brushes, Anna caught a glimpse of the QR codes she'd been affixing to each item. She really was as organized as she looked. A true professional. This should never have happened to her.

"This place is gorgeous." Sammy looked around the shop. "Why haven't I been here before?"

Angela shrugged gracefully and raised an eyebrow. "Good question. Why haven't you?" Then her smile dropped. "I hope I'll still be able to attract customers after what happened. Who would come to a winery that kills people?"

"Now, don't think like that," Anna said briskly. "Your winery doesn't kill people, and you're still going to get plenty of customers. Like Sammy said, this place really is gorgeous. Did you do all this yourself?"

"It's taken me six years to get to this point." Angela leaned forward onto the serving counter. "I didn't start from scratch. I bought an existing winery, but they were growing more traditional New Jersey grapes. I've been experimenting—improving the wine, I hope."

Anna and Angela pulled up a couple of the tall stools that lined the customer side of the counter and jumped up. "Tell me more, Angela. How did you get into this business?"

Angela laughed. "Not a normal choice, I know. My parents thought I was crazy when I told them I was getting my degree in viticulture."

"I didn't even know you could get a degree in winemaking," Sammy said.

"Not a lot of schools offer it, but I got into a good program. In upstate New York, which was great because I was trained in growing and producing wines in a cold climate. I know I've been lucky—I had some money I could invest in this place—but I've worked hard to get it to this point, very hard."

"I get it," Anna said with feeling. "I know how much work is involved in running a business—and it's not all glamorous." She grimaced, picturing the well-used laundry room in her basement.

"So, I used what I knew about business and working with people combined with what I learned about winemaking, and I turned an old winery around."

"What do you mean 'turned it around'?" Anna asked. "You mentioned the grapes. What did you change?"

"Come on." Angela pushed away from the counter. "I'll show you."

She led the women out through a wide door at the back of the shop. Anna saw the tank room to their right, but Angela turned left and led them back outside to the covered patio. They crossed the patio and stepped right into the vineyard. Anna ran a hand along the vines, still covered with thick, juicy bunches of grapes.

"You haven't harvested your grapes yet?"

"Some we have. Some we haven't," Angela explained. "It depends on the type of grape and what we plan to do with it."

She stopped and waved a hand to take in the expanse of vines. "I have thirty acres here. It's on the small side for a working winery but kind of typical in this part of the state. Bordeaux grapes tend to grow best in this soil. It's a loamy sand soil with lots of gravel. So I grow Cabernet Sauvignon." Angela pointed at different sections of the vines as she identified them. "Cabernet Franc, Merlot, Tempranillo, Sauvignon Blanc, Sémillon, and Muscadelle." As she spoke about her grapes, her eyes lingered on each section. Taking in their condition, perhaps. Maybe looking for issues. Always at work.

"But you've already harvested some?" Anna asked.

Angela nodded. "I start harvesting the Tempranillo in August. Those are the grapes scheduled for sparkling wines. The other grapes need a little longer on the vines, though I'll tell you, determining exactly when to harvest them is as much an art as a science. This time of year, I'm watching the weather forecast like a crazy person!" She laughed then sobered. "I don't know if I'll even be able to manage the harvest this year."

"I'm sure you will." Anna put an arm around her. "I'll do whatever I can to help. Tell me more about the process. What was James doing when he died?"

Angela nodded her thanks. "Back inside, then." The trio trooped back into the barn that held the wine-making equipment. They passed into a room full of giant stainless-steel tanks. The high ceiling of the barn let plenty of air circulate in the room, and Anna could hear the hum of a powerful air circulation system.

"These are the smaller tanks." Angela ran a caressing hand along two tanks that were, indeed, less than half the size of the others. Each of the tanks had a short ladder running up the side.

"You said he was stirring the wine. What's that about? I had no idea you had to stir the wine," Sammy said.

"You don't have to. In fact, for most of our wines, we don't. But I like to experiment, and I'd mentioned that to James. Stirring the lees is an old tradition that I decided to try. It can add stability, body, and flavor to the wine. But it's notoriously dangerous, too, because it releases more carbon dioxide." Angela pulled her hands away from the tank, and Anna could practically see her mind working—questioning, asking, wondering if she was, in fact, to blame. Angela shook her head. "We remove the lid to stir it." She nodded toward a large metal stirrer that looked like a perforated paddle. "That increases the risk, since you're right there, leaning over it."

"You stir the lees?" Anna asked.

"Right, sorry. The lees are basically yeast particles that are left over from the fermentation process. When you stir the wine, you stir those lees from the bottom of the tank back into the body of the wine. If done right, they can add extra flavor and texture to the wine, particularly sparkling wine, which this will soon be." Angela's eyes glowed with pride as she described the process.

Anna felt a pang of jealousy—Sammy had her bakery. Angela had her wine. *What do I have?* A houseful of dirty linen and toilets that needed scrubbing. At that moment, she realized how much she missed the creative aspect of doing her research, coming up with new ideas and new explanations for human behavior. Not to mention talking with people, listening to their stories, figuring out what motivated them and how they lived. *Well, Anna,* she told herself, *right now, figuring out how James Longhurst died will have to be your main focus.* She could think about her other choices another time.

"So, you don't stir all your wine?" Sammy was asking.

Angela shook her head. "Each varietal has a slightly different process. I sell some as single grape wines. Others I blend."

Anna took a breath and looked around the room. "The air seems perfectly fresh to me."

"It is!" Angela threw up her hands. "I put so much money and time into making sure my ventilation system was top-of-the-line. Everyone who comes in here to work gets an oxygen meter." Angela walked over to a shelf next to the main door, stocked with a row of bright-yellow plastic devices the size and shape of walkie-talkies. Each meter rested in a bracket that was connected to a power outlet in the wall, charging up while waiting its turn. Angela picked up the first in the row and held it out so Anna could see the battery indicator. A small QR code on the bottom of the unit emphasized the seriousness with which Angela took her business. "Anyone who comes in, first thing they do is pick up one of these. Once one is used, it goes to the back of the line to make sure it's fully charged before anyone picks it up again."

"So how did he die?" Sammy asked.

Angela shrugged. "Something went wrong."

"Sounds like multiple things went wrong," Anna corrected her. "The ventilation system wasn't working, so no fresh air was getting in."

"And his oxygen meter failed to warn him." Angela let out a loud huff. "I told him it was dangerous. A carbon dioxide concentration as low as eight percent is enough to kill a person."

"I still don't understand why you let him back here." Sammy's phone started to buzz. "Sorry, excuse me." She stepped away from the other women as she answered it quietly.

Angela smiled sadly. "Like I said, he was a friend. A longtime family friend. In fact, I'm going to go see Isabelle later today."

"Isabelle?"

"His wife. Oh, I should say his widow. She's staying at the Restful Retreat Inn for a few days before heading back to Stone Harbor." Angela looked around the room, her expression vague, her pain reflected in her eyes. "I wanted to be nice. He loved wine as much as I do. We had that in common. I knew I could trust him in here... at least, I thought I could."

"Sorry, Angela, Anna, I gotta run." Sammy walked toward the exit even as she spoke.

"Is everything okay? What happened?" Anna asked, walking after her friend.

"Just something at work. I need to get back." She paused and looked back at Anna. "I am sorry Angela, but it's kind of urgent."

Anna turned and jogged back toward Angela. She put her hands on Angela's shoulders and looked her in the eye. "This wasn't your fault, Angela. I'm sure of it. Everything you've showed us today just proves how careful you are and how well you know your tools. Plus, I know you. I know the way you run your business, and I don't believe it for a second. Someone messed with your equipment. This wasn't a tragic accident. It was murder." She gave her shoulders one more squeeze then ran to catch up to Sammy.

"Ahem."

Anna turned from the table at the cough. "Oh! Hi."

Luke stood in the doorway of the kitchen, and he looked fabulous. It turned out he cleaned up even better than Anna had expected. He'd shaved off the light stubble that usually covered his chin, and somehow it made his jaw look even squarer, his eyes greener. He wore a black cotton long-sleeve shirt that looked so soft Anna wanted to run her hands along it. His shirt was neatly tucked into khaki pants, but he'd rolled his sleeves up partway, keeping the look casual.

Anna glanced down at herself as she patted Eoin on the head. She'd just served Eoin and his babysitter, Trish, their dinner—which involved simply opening the pizza box and providing them each with a plate and napkins. She'd managed to avoid getting any tomato sauce on herself, which was a good start, particularly since her mind was on Sammy and whatever problem she was dealing with.

Sammy had refused to talk about it, changing the

conversation to what Anna was going to wear that night. Right now, she was glad she'd taken Sammy's advice. Her dark jeans paired with the loose white cotton shirt over a white tank top matched Luke's style perfectly. She'd even let Sammy put her into strappy sandals with a bit of a heel.

Just to see who had been right about the heels argument, Anna walked over and pecked Luke on the cheek. *Well, shoot, Sammy was right!* Even with the heels, Luke still stood a few inches taller than Anna.

"Hi." Luke reacted to her greeting with a grin. "You look great."

Trish, the teenage daughter of a neighbor, giggled and rolled her eyes. Eoin looked confused but laughed with her anyway.

"Okay, you two." Anna hurried back to the table to give Eoin one more hug. "Thank you again, Trish, for being available on such short notice. I'm sure Eoin will be a little angel for you. Won't you?" She gave Eoin a hard look.

He nodded, tomato sauce already dripping down his chin. Anna wiped it away with a napkin before following Luke out of the house.

"Let's take the long way round." Luke led her down toward the beach.

"Sure," Anna agreed, not actually knowing where they were taking the long way to. But it was a beautiful evening, and Anna was always up for a walk on the beach.

The sky had just begun its transformation, pink and orange hues spreading out over the dark-green water. A few hardy beachgoers still huddled on chairs, wrapped in towels and blankets to enjoy the last light of the day. More people had made the same choice as Luke and Anna, and they passed other couples walking hand in hand along the water.

Luke glanced at her, offering one of his familiar grins, but didn't reach out to take her hand. In a way, Anna was relieved. That might have been too weird. It was *Luke*, after all.

They walked in silence for a few minutes, taking in the colorful expanse of sky over the water, the comforting scents of the ocean carried on the light breeze, the sound of the water gently lapping against the beach. The gulls were already prepared for the night, standing in small groups up the beach, heads tucked close into their bodies, facing into the wind.

"I visited Angela's winery with Sammy today." Anna finally broke the silence, voicing the thoughts that had been running through her head. "She's concerned about whether or not she'll be able to keep her business running now."

"I bet." Luke nodded. "A death on the premises is not good for business." He walked closer to her and bumped her slightly. "But you already know that."

"I surely do." Anna laughed. "But I got over it, and I told Angela she will too. We just need to figure out how James died so people don't think Angela was somehow responsible."

Luke nodded again. "If it was an accident, she could be held accountable. I don't know if that would mean charges or fines or what, but she's responsible for making sure her equipment is all up to code."

"Exactly. But if someone messed with the equipment..."

Luke laughed out loud. "You're looking for a murderer? Again?"

Anna shrugged and felt herself blush. "It's not that I'm hoping there's a killer out there. I just want to understand how this could have happened. I mean really. Too many things would have had to break down at exactly the same time for this to have been an accident."

"And if it wasn't an accident, then Angela isn't to blame."

"Exactly." Anna beamed up at Luke, reached out, and took his hand.

He held hers tentatively at first then wrapped his fingers around hers. "So let the police do their job. If someone else tampered with her equipment, there will be evidence. Fingerprints, DNA, that sort of thing."

Anna snorted then bit down on her lips. "Sorry. It's just that DNA evidence isn't as easy to gather—or test—as some people think. It can take weeks, even months, for DNA results to come back. And that's if they even find any evidence sufficient to capture DNA. If the person who messed with Angela's equipment wore gloves and didn't happen to have any hairs fall out while he was doing it, there won't be any DNA."

"Okay," Luke said tensely. "No DNA. But they could still find fingerprints." Anna opened her mouth to reply, but Luke got there first. "Unless he wore gloves."

Anna raised her eyebrows and nodded. They'd apparently reached the end of their stroll on the beach. Luke guided Anna up the beach with his hand on the small of her back. They followed the side street up another block to a pub tucked around the corner from Washington Mall, the town's main street.

They settled into a cozy booth, Luke with a beer and Anna with a glass of white wine. Anna glanced around, wondering why she hadn't been there before. It was small but comfortable with a mellow atmosphere, clearly a place designed for locals rather than tourists. Black marks on the low wood beams over the bar spoke to the days when smoking had been allowed inside. The absence of signs on the door that Luke pointed out as the restroom served as another indicator that this place catered to regulars, not one-time visitors. Luke had greeted their waitress by name and didn't even bother to look at his menu.

"What do you recommend?" Anna ran her eyes over her own menu.

"That depends. What are you in the mood for?"

Anna shrugged. "Um.... how's their tuna steak?"

Luke shook his head. "You don't want that. In a place like this, you're better off getting something with red meat."

"Even at the shore?" Anna laughed. "The fish must at least be fresh here."

"Trust me. Go with red meat."

Anna took him at his word, ordering a burger after Luke had ordered a New York strip steak.

As she sipped her wine, her mind turned back to the problem of Angela and her winery. "How can I prove that this wasn't negligence on Angela's part? How do I show that someone tampered with her equipment?" Her words mirrored her thoughts, but the surprise on Luke's face told her his mind had been somewhere completely different.

"Like I said before, you need evidence." Luke shrugged. "I know you said there wouldn't be fingerprints or DNA, but the police must have other proof they look for."

Anna nodded, thinking. "Motive and opportunity are a good start. Who would want James dead?"

Luke laughed out loud. "That's not evidence. That's just guessing."

"Oh." Anna thought about that. In a way, Luke was right. Maybe she should be focusing her attention on finding hard evidence instead of digging into clues like motives and schedules and shared secrets. Then she shook her head. "But if you have enough clues, even if each on its own isn't sufficient, they can paint a pretty clear picture."

Luke didn't disagree, but his skepticism was painted on his face.

Anna dropped the topic as their food arrived. One bite told her that Luke was right about the place. Their food was amazing—well, at least their meat dishes. She couldn't help but wonder how the tuna would have tasted.

Their conversation over dinner stayed away from death and murder. They talked about the house, mostly, something they both loved. Luke spoke with pride about the work he'd done, and Anna had to agree. They shared ideas for ways to improve the ground floor, something Anna hadn't even thought about tackling.

When Anna ordered a second glass of wine, the bartender came over with the bottle. Greeting Luke as a friend, he tipped the bottle over Anna's glass, and she recognized the White Pine Winery label as he poured.

"You serve local wine here?" Anna asked with a smile. "That's great."

"Sure," the bartender grunted. "Angela's done a lot for this town through her work at the small business association. All she asks is that we serve her wine in return."

Anna took another sip, more thoughtfully this time. The wine was a little rough around the edges, but it tasted bright and clean and left an almost-sweet taste on her tongue. "Not bad for a Jersey wine." She smiled.

The bartender grunted again but this time with a frown. "Thanks, I think."

"You're thinking about how to prove this was murder again, aren't you?" Luke asked after his friend had returned to his place behind the bar.

Anna shrugged. "Of course. I just don't know what to look for. Like you said, I can talk to people, find out who has a motive, but I don't know the equipment she uses. I wouldn't be able to tell if something had been tampered with or not." She looked up at Luke and batted her eyes. "But you could."

Luke laughed, a long, deep laugh that Anna couldn't help but join. It felt good to relax, to let go. Regardless of whether Luke was laughing at her or with her.

He finally controlled his laughter enough to respond. "I could. I can take a look if you want. Don't get me wrong, I still think you should be leaving it to the police. But if you are going to get involved, I'm glad you're going to do what I said—look for real evidence. It's the only way to prove anything."

Anna nodded and smiled, but inside she wondered, *Did I just agree to do what Luke said?* There she'd thought she was asking him for help, not instructions.

$$\clubsuit \quad 8 \quad \clubsuit$$

Night had fallen by the time they left the pub, and they walked home through town, skirting the main shopping street and choosing quieter side streets. As they walked, they passed through circles of light cast by low lamps designed to look like traditional gas lamps. The shift in lighting mimicked the fluctuations in Anna's thoughts, from brightness to shadows then back again.

"Do you really think I shouldn't be involved in figuring out what happened at Angela's winery?" She finally asked the question that had been bugging her for the past hour.

Luke looked at her, surprised. "You're still thinking about that?" He shrugged. "You know I don't like you getting involved in murder investigations. It's too dangerous. But since this isn't a murder investigation..." He shrugged again then reached out to wrap an arm around her shoulders.

She leaned into him, bumping hips as they walked. He felt strong, safe. She let herself wallow in the warm comfort he provided but only for a few minutes. "I think it was murder, though." She straightened and pulled away. "I know Angela, and I don't believe she'd let her equipment get to the point where it would break down like that."

"If she did, that was pretty negligent," Luke agreed.

"And Angela is definitely not negligent. Something else happened there, and I need to help her figure out what."

They hadn't passed many people on the streets as they walked. Those they did see were mostly tourists strolling through the historic streets, looking around, wide-eyed and smiling as they absorbed the beauty and history of the town. That made the figure hurrying toward them stand out.

As the person got closer, Anna barely recognized Angela. Her silky hair fell loose from the clip at the back of her head, half of it still up while the other half trailed artlessly along her shoulders. She held a soggy tissue up to her face, and her shoulders shook as she sobbed and scurried along.

"Angela, wait." Anna put out her hands to catch the woman as she passed by without acknowledging them.

Angela jerked away from Anna's touch then looked up and recognized her friend. "Oh, Anna." She burst into tears again and fell into Anna's arms.

Anna's eyes widened as she looked at Luke in confusion but leaned in close to comfort Angela. She let Angela cry for a moment, hugging her tightly.

When Angela had regained control, Anna stepped back. "What happened? Are you okay?"

Angela shook her head as she dabbed at her eyes with the tissue. When she realized it was already soggy, she looked at it in disgust, thrust it into a pocket, and pulled a clean tissue out of her purse. "I'm sorry, but I just got terrible news."

"Are you okay?" Anna asked again. "Is it someone in your family?"

Angela managed a weak smile. "You could almost say that. It's the winery."

"Something *else* happened at the winery?" Luke asked. "Now what?"

Angela's lower lip trembled, and tears gathered in her eyes, but she blinked repeatedly and took a deep breath. "I just met with my broker. I'm selling the place."

"What?" Anna's tone carried all the shock she felt at the news. "But why?"

Angela shook her head, clearly at a loss, and looked up at the sky to control her tears and emotions. "It's no use. It's almost crush—harvest time, I mean. I haven't sold a single bottle of wine since the accident. And now I can't get my usual crew to come in for the harvest. Word's got around that my winery isn't safe." She gulped loudly then let her tears loose.

This time, Luke pulled her close to comfort her. She leaned into him, putting a hand on his shoulder as she cried.

"Oh, Angela, I'm so sorry." Anna watched her friend cry, hating her feeling of helplessness. "Is this a done deal? Are you sure?"

Angela nodded against Luke's shoulder. "My broker will be working on the details over the next few days, then he'll post the announcement. I don't even know who would want to buy the place now. And my grapes." She let out a wail and burst into fresh tears.

Anna stood silently and took in her friend's pain. Luke patted Angela uncomfortably on the back until she sniffled and straightened up.

"Thank you." She dabbed Luke's black shirt with her tissue, failing to sop up the wet patches she'd left behind.

"Angela, I can't stand to see you like this," Anna said. "There must be something we can do."

"Can we go back in time and warn James that my equipment isn't safe?" Angela asked dryly.

"No." Anna kept her voice calm. "But we can go forward in time and prove that your equipment *is* safe. I don't believe for a second his death was the result of you not taking care of your winery. I know how much work you put into that place. I'm sure something else happened."

"You really think someone tampered with my equipment? But that's a terrible thought."

Anna nodded. "It is. It means someone wanted James dead. Or—" Anna's eyes widened as she had another thought. "Or they thought you would be the next person stirring the wine. Maybe James wasn't the intended victim at all."

9

"Thanks again for coming so quickly." Anna used the back of her hand to wipe a stray hair out of her eyes then grabbed a dishcloth to dry her palms.

"Really... not a... problem," Luke grunted. He slid out from under the sink and grinned up at her. "I told you I'm here whenever you need me."

With a burp and a gurgle, the water started draining.

"Thank goodness," Anna said with feeling, looking at the stack of breakfast dishes she'd piled next to the clogged sink. "At least now I can get to work on those."

"You sure do know how to have a good time." Luke laughed as he stood and leaned back against the counter. "Any coffee left?"

"I'll make you some fresh." Anna lit the ring under the kettle then reached for the grinder. Once the French press was full and brewing, she carried it over to the table to join Luke.

Just as she sat, her phone rang. "Huh, that's weird." She glanced at the caller ID. "I'm so sorry. I need to get this. It's one of my former professors. I can't imagine why he's calling." Anna grabbed the phone and walked through to the lounge. "Peter, hi. It's good to hear from you—a bit of a surprise."

"Anna, I'm glad I caught you. I don't know if you heard the news yet." Peter's voice sounded strained, but then, as Anna recalled, it always had. Most of the faculty at the university where she had been close to finishing her PhD were always under immense pressure.

"Um, no. What news?"

Peter laughed nervously, and Anna felt her grip on her phone tighten.

"What happened?" she asked.

"Well, it's about Steve Upton."

Anna very carefully loosened her grip on the phone before she broke it—or her fingers. The mention of her ex-boyfriend—who had also been her dissertation advisor—meant it was not going to be good news. "Tell me."

"He's just lost his teaching position here. Plagiarism."

Anna's knees buckled under her, and she reached out with one hand to steady herself enough to drop onto the sofa instead of onto the floor. Tough Cookie let out a sharp meow as she moved out of Anna's way. "Finally. So they believe me?"

"Oh." Peter paused. "Well, we always believed you, Anna. But no, this was another case. He was caught plagiarizing in a published work, quite baldly."

"He was caught again," Anna said through gritted teeth. "Caught *again*. I caught him last time too."

"Of course. Right. Yes." Peter stumbled over the words. "Well, I was sure you'd want to know. Perhaps this might give you the encouragement you need?"

"Encouragement? For what?"

"Well, to come back of course. It hasn't been too long.

You wouldn't need to retake any courses or exams. Just form a new committee and get to work writing up your research."

Anna looked out through the large lounge window into the yard and street beyond as she let her hand run through Tough Cookie's black-and-white fur. She'd faced that question so many times. She'd left her research out of anger and frustration. Her advisor—who was also her secret boyfriend—had stolen her research and published it under his name. And when she'd publicly accused him of it, her accusations had received a less-than-satisfying reception.

"Anna, are you there?"

"Yes. Yes, sorry." Anna blinked. "I was just thinking. Look, Peter, thank you so much for calling me. I appreciate knowing."

"So you'll consider my suggestion? I'd be happy to take on the role of your advisor if you do return. You know I'm fascinated by the way you traced the use of Pueblan remedies in Philly communities."

"I can't tell you how glad I am to hear that. I would love to work with you, Peter. Your research has always inspired me. But let me think about it, okay?"

After promising to get back to him soon, Anna tossed the phone onto the end table and leaned back against the sofa. Just as she sat back, the standing lamp in the corner near the window blinked off and on. Anna blew out a breath of frustration and walked over to jiggle the lamp. She loved the lamp—it had been part of that room for as long as Anna could remember—but something was clearly not working right.

When she shook it, it stopped blinking. Probably not the best way to repair it, but it would suffice for the time being. She had other things to worry about—like getting a better lampshade for it. The one she'd recently purchased to replace the old, worn-out shade was not working for her at all. A glittery-gold fringe lined the high-gloss, cotton-candy-pink shade. It looked more garish than antique.

She put her hands on her hips and turned to look around the rest of the room. *What else am I putting off?* she wondered. *How many more projects do I have to take care of, and will it ever end?*

"Bad news?" Luke pushed through the door from the kitchen.

Anna turned her head to look at him. "Not exactly. Actually, kind of good news. Steve— you remember my ex?"

Luke nodded. "Sure, how could I forget?"

"Well, he finally got the punishment he deserved. He's lost his position at the university. And after that, it's unlikely anyone else will hire him."

"Hmm." Luke nodded thoughtfully. "Is that important to you?"

Anna grinned. "No, it's not. You know, I haven't thought about him in weeks."

"Not since you tried to pin a murder on him?" Luke laughed.

"Exactly." Anna laughed with him. "Not since then."

Luke looked down for a moment, his foot toying with the edge of the rug, then back at Anna. "I couldn't help but overhear some of your conversation. It sounded like you're thinking about going back to school."

Anna raised her eyebrows as she shrugged. "It's just something to think about. Peter, one of my professors, offered to serve as my advisor if I do go back, which is pretty cool. It's nice to know at least one person out there values my research."

Luke grinned as he shook his head. "You know Steve did, too, enough to steal it."

Anna tossed a throw pillow at him, which he caught easily.

"Hey, I'm pretty sure you're not supposed to throw the throw pillows."

"I don't know what I'm going to do, Luke. I love it here. But I do miss the work…" She thought about that pang of jealousy she'd felt at the winery, the desire to have something to create, to own. Then she thought about how much more work she had to do around Climbing Rose Cottage.

"If you love it here so much, then don't go." Luke shrugged. "It's simple. Plus, I don't want you to leave." He raised an eyebrow as he looked down at her.

Anna shut her eyes as she shook her head. "I do tend to make things more complicated than they need to be, don't I? Oh." She opened her eyes. "Did I mention my mom is coming down today?"

"Your mother? No, you didn't mention that. And that's my cue to cut out of here. I'm not great with meeting the parents." He tossed the pillow back at her as he spoke.

Anna laughed. "It's just my mom, Luke. But seriously." She walked with him to the door. "Thank you so much for coming over. You're a lifesaver."

"Not a problem. You don't go back to school, and I'll make it a habit." He leaned over and gave her a chaste kiss on the cheek. Then, glancing around to see that no guests were around, he kissed her lightly on the lips.

Anna felt herself blush, and her face broke into a broad smile. "See you soon?"

"Absolutely," Luke called as he left.

Anna watched him saunter down the path to the sidewalk before closing the door. She still had chores to get done and afternoon tea to prep. She took a deep breath. Luke was a handsome man, no question about that. She paused for a moment and thought about what he had said.

A meow brought her attention down to the cat wrapping itself around her legs. "What?" She leaned down and picked up Tough Cookie. "What are you saying? That I still have a murder to investigate? Don't worry. I already know my next step."

Tough Cookie meowed again and rubbed her head against Anna's shoulder.

"Now what?" She put her ear to Tough Cookie's face. "He is a handsome man? You're right. He is." She snuggled her face deep into the cat's fur as she smiled then frowned. "I just wish he'd stop telling me what to do."

10

Anna walked the half mile from Climbing Rose Cottage to the Restful Retreat Inn, approaching it from the town rather than along Beach Avenue. The residential streets were quiet, as most visitors tended to congregate near the beach or Washington Mall, so she used the time to focus on her pretext for showing up at the inn unexpectedly. She'd met the owner a few times but hadn't had a chance to talk to him at length. *Will he believe I'm dropping by, unannounced, in the middle of an August morning, to talk about running a hotel in Cape May?*

When she turned onto Trenton Avenue toward the beach, the expanse of sky and ocean opened in front of her. By the time she'd walked the final block to the inn, she felt like she was no longer in a town at all. She paused at the corner, taking a deep breath of sea air, listening to the calls of the gulls that circled overhead. From where she stood, she could just see the ocean over the dunes but not the families that she knew were gathered on the beach beyond. It was as if she were alone with the sea and sky. Definitely a good location for the Restful Retreat Inn.

She took a moment to focus her thoughts and strengthen her resolve then marched up to the front door. As she raised a hand to knock, she saw the door stood partially open. She pushed it gently, and it swung wide, so she stepped into the front hall.

She wasn't sure what she had expected from the Restful Retreat Inn, but what she saw was definitely not it. The wide-open foyer she'd anticipated based on the architecture of the house had been transformed into a cozy entrance with wood and plaster paneling. The soft browns and pale greens of the walls served as perfect backdrops for calming paintings of the ocean that waited just outside. The soft tinkle of a fountain complemented the soothing music coming from hidden speakers. Scents of eucalyptus commingled with those of the fresh flowers placed artistically around the vestibule. She took a breath, and her shoulders relaxed. *Wow, this place works!*

"May I help you?"

Anna turned to the voice, realizing that one of the brown walls actually held a tall desk, behind which stood a woman. She smiled in greeting but had the air of a clinician rather than a receptionist. Her dark hair was pulled back into a tight bun, and she wore a pale-green cotton jacket reminiscent of a lab coat that hung loosely over her white pants and shirt.

"Oh, hi." Anna clasped her hands in front of her and tried not to look nervous. "I'm looking for Mark. Is he around?" Anna tossed out the first name of the inn's owner as if they were the best of friends.

The woman frowned. "Mark, the owner?" She shook her head. "It's Wednesday. He's up in... I'm sorry, who are you?"

Anna smiled and held out a hand. "Anna McGregor. I own Climbing Rose Cottage. I know Mark from the Small

Business Association. I was passing and had a few questions I wanted to run by him. Sorry to just show up unannounced like this."

"I thought you looked familiar." The woman reached for the datebook that lay open on the desk. "I think I've seen you at some of those meetings. I'm sorry he's not here. I can leave a note for him, if that would help."

"That would be great, thank you. Listen, would it be okay if I took a tiny peek around? Since I'm here..." Anna smiled hopefully at the woman, who frowned back at her.

"We have clients here. I can't let you do anything that would disturb them."

"Oh no, of course not. I completely respect that. I would be as silent as a mouse. I just really wanted to see this place. Mark has said so much about it. I can almost picture it." Anna crossed her fingers behind her back at the white lie.

"Well... I guess that would be all right. Since you're a friend?" She said the last statement as a clear question.

"Thank you. I appreciate it." Anna didn't wait for the woman to reconsider, stepping toward one door in the hall then looking questioningly at the woman.

"That's the lounge." The woman nodded as she spoke. "The spa is through there."

"Thanks!" Anna pushed the door open and slid through.

The lounge of the Victorian mansion had been as thoroughly modernized as the foyer. Where Anna's featured classic eighteenth-century furniture, window coverings, and art, the inn's room was light, bright, and airy, continuing the color scheme from the front hall. Large windows faced the ocean across the street, providing a perfect vista of sunlight glittering on the blue-green waves. Three people lay in comfortable lounging chairs dotted around the room, wrapped in terry cloth robes and with glasses of cucumber-and-herb water. They all looked entirely relaxed and peaceful. The inn was doing its job well.

Anna tiptoed as silently as she could over to the far door and slipped into the spa. That room's windows were covered in heavy fabric that blocked the sun, but low lights scattered along the ceiling and floor kept the dimness to a comfortable glow. Two more people sat in chairs along the wall, presumably waiting their turn. As Anna stood, taking in the atmosphere and letting her eyes adjust to the dimness, another woman in a pale-green jacket came through a curtain in the far wall.

"Adam?" she whispered.

The man waiting in a robe stood, ready for his massage.

The masseuse glanced at Anna. "Are you here for a treatment?"

"No, sorry," Anna whispered back, recognizing the need to keep her voice low. "I'm looking for Isabelle—Isabelle Longhurst? Is she here?"

The woman gestured back to the room Anna had just passed through. "She finished a few minutes ago. She's relaxing in the lounge."

"Oh, sorry. I must have missed her." Anna grimaced and backed out of the dark room.

In the lounge, she blinked in the light for a moment before focusing on the people in the room. One was a man, so Anna felt fairly confident he was not the recently widowed Isabelle Paige Longhurst. That left two women. One looked far too young to have been married to James Longhurst, but the other looked far too old. Figuring money had its privileges, Anna approached the younger woman. While James had been in his sixties, the woman could easily pass for forty.

"Isabelle?" she asked quietly, perching on a nearby chair.

The robed woman blinked as if she'd been dreaming and turned to Anna. "Yes. Can I help you?"

"I'm sorry to bother you. I'm Anna McGregor. I run a B and B here in town." She leaned farther forward on her chair, lowering her voice even more. "I was so sorry to hear about what happened to your husband."

"James? Oh, thank you." Isabelle slid a little higher in her chair, adjusting her terry cloth robe. As she moved, Anna noticed the spots on her hands, the loose skin around her neck, that told her the woman wasn't as young as she looked, just very well cared for. "Did you know James? I'm sorry. If we've met before, I simply don't remember."

"No, no, that's fine." Anna offered a friendly smile. "I'm friends with Angela Nelson, who owns the winery. I can only imagine how distressing this must be for you."

"Yes, thank you." Isabelle sank back down into her chair and closed her eyes.

"The thing is." Anna ignored the obvious dismissal. "Angela is very concerned about what might have really happened to James."

Isabelle's eyes opened then narrowed. "What really happened? What are you talking about? The foolish man took a risk he shouldn't have and paid the price." She pushed herself back up on her chair, grunting a little at the effort. "He's paid a high price for his wine fetish for long enough."

"Wine fetish?"

"Well, it might as well be. Every dime we have he would put into that wine business of his. And I use the term 'business' loosely, I assure you." She stretched a thin arm out for the water on the table next to her chair and took a dainty sip.

Anna paused, not sure how to respond. The woman was grieving, and Anna knew everybody grieved in different ways. Anger at the dead person was not uncommon. Isabelle's words struck her as inappropriate, regardless, if not downright strange. "He knew a lot about wine, though, didn't he?"

"Of course." Isabelle nodded. "He spent his entire life learning about wine. It was all he loved." She lowered her eyes and picked at her robe.

"I'm so sorry," Anna repeated, thinking furiously.

"Don't be. This is just the shock I needed to make some changes." Isabelle looked back up at Anna and smiled. "I'm finally free—to do what I want with whomever I want." She gave Anna a knowing wink and leaned back in her chair.

"Oh, I see. Well..." Anna looked around the comfortable room. "I'm glad you're able to take some time for yourself now. I'm sure that helps. You live not far from here, right?"

"I do. But it's so peaceful here." She raised her water. "Everything I need at my fingertips. Much better than going back to that empty house." She made a dismayed face.

"Of course, I'm sure it would be distressing there."

"Distressing? Oh no." Isabelle laughed merrily. "It's just that here I have people to take care of me." She raised the water as if in a toast and took another sip.

The door from the front hall opened. Anna noticed a man slide in but didn't pay him much attention, her mind still spinning with questions she wanted to ask Isabelle. "How long—"

"There you are!" The man's sharp call cut Anna off mid-question. "I went up to your room looking for you." He crouched down in front of Isabelle, a hand resting on her leg. "How are you doing today, Mother?" He glanced at Anna, his eyes running up and down as he took in her windblown mass of red hair, well-worn jeans, and casual T-shirt. "And who, exactly, are you?"

11

Anna took a calming breath, letting the breeze off the ocean do its work. Isabelle's son stood next to her, looking out over the water as if trying to spot land. At least he wasn't talking.

Ralph Longhurst hadn't stopped talking from the moment he'd walked in and found Anna with his mother. His tone had attracted the attention of the clerk, who'd immediately shuttled Anna out of the inn with promises to let Mark know she'd been there. For reasons she didn't understand, Ralph had left with her.

In his late thirties or early forties, he was dressed casually in dark denim jeans and a cotton button-down shirt with the sleeves rolled up. Anna could see the creases where his jeans had been ironed and couldn't help but wonder what kind of person ironed their jeans. A paunch had formed at his waistline, but he otherwise seemed to be keeping in shape. Except for the skinny arms that poked out from his rolled-up sleeves. Not a man who engaged in much hard labor, Anna suspected.

"Thanks for walking me out, Mr. Longhurst. I'm surprised you didn't want to stay with your mother."

"Call me Ralph, please. I was just popping in before heading home. Didn't plan to stay. Just wanted to make sure she was okay." He nodded as he kept his eyes on the ocean. "She looked okay to me."

"She did." Anna agreed. "I'm glad you're here, though. I was hoping to talk with you too."

"Really?" Ralph dragged his gaze away from the water to look at her. "About what?"

Anna chose her words carefully. "I was so sorry to hear about your father. He sounds like a fascinating man. I wish I could have known him."

Ralph nodded, and Anna saw the muscles in his jaw moving as he bit down—to keep his emotions in check, perhaps. She stayed silent, letting him deal with his grief.

"He was a good man," Ralph finally said. "I'm still mad at him. I can't believe he made such a basic mistake. He knew better."

"That's what I wanted to talk to you about. What if it wasn't a mistake?"

Ralph nodded. "Negligence, you mean. Yes, I've thought of that a lot, but Angela has been a friend of the family for years. I would never sue her." He raised an interrogative eyebrow. "Wait, I thought you said you were friends with Angela."

"I am, and I wasn't implying negligence at all. In fact, I'm wondering if something else was going on entirely."

"Something else? Hmm. It's funny you should say that." As he spoke, he turned and walked along the beach, back toward the center of town. He walked awkwardly, with jerking movements, skipping over patches of sand that looked too wet or too soft, sidestepping others.

Anna fell into place beside him, doing her best to avoid him when he skipped in her direction.

"Like I said," Ralph continued, "I just don't believe Dad would make a mistake like that. But what else could have happened?"

"We know his oxygen meter wasn't working," Anna pointed out. "What if that wasn't accidental? What if someone broke it intentionally?"

Ralph's eyes opened wide. "Yes! That would explain it." He lowered his brows. "But why would you even think that? You said you ran a B and B."

"I do. I'm just a friend of Angela's, trying to help. She's so upset about your father's death, and she's concerned that something in her winery wasn't working properly. I want to help her."

Ralph didn't respond right away, so they walked a few awkward paces in silence. Finally, Ralph nodded. "Then I want to help too. What can I tell you?"

"Oh." Anna was taken aback by his enthusiasm. She hadn't expected him to understand her involvement, let alone offer to help. "What can you tell me about your father?"

"He loved wine. I can tell you that." Ralph smiled sadly then looked away and blinked a few times. He took a deep breath. "Sorry, I miss him so much. I didn't expect to be this upset."

"You didn't expect to be upset at your father's death?"

Ralph laughed. "It sounds horrible when you say it like that. I just mean... Dad and I argued a lot."

"About what?"

"Wine, what else?" Ralph laughed again, this time sadly. "Dad was an oenophile through and through. He loved wine. He loved reading about it, learning about it, visiting vineyards, getting involved in the process of making it. He loved it with a passion."

"How did he get into the winemaking business?"

"Oh, he wasn't in the winemaking business. In fact, he wasn't really in it for the business at all. He spent thirty years on Wall Street, working at a hedge fund. He picked up his love for wine somewhere along the way, so when he decided he'd had enough of Wall Street, he retired and started poking around wineries. Soon enough, he got his license to import. He basically tootled around wineries in Chile, Italy, France, and Spain and made arrangements with the winemakers to ship their wines to the States and sell them here."

"He sold the wines?"

Ralph shook his head. "Nope. All he did was import them. That's it. Well, he did make a little bit of wine on his own. He set up a small press and vat in the back of my warehouse, bought local grapes, and fermented them there." Ralph made a face. "It's not very good though. I think that was why he liked visiting Angela's winery, to learn more about the process of making it."

"So you're the distributor?"

"That's right. I built up a business based on Dad's hobby." He laughed ruefully. "To be honest, I run the business side of Dad's importing company too."

"Were you involved in the choices he made?"

"Oh no. Dad wouldn't let anyone else get involved in that. It was all his. His tastes, his preferences. He didn't care whether the wine he was importing would sell well or not. He wasn't in it for the money. At least now I can change that."

"You'll take over the import business?"

"Hmm, I don't know about that. I could make deals with other importers, find wines that will really sell, invest more in the business. That was one of the things we fought about."

"What?"

"Putting more money into the business. Dad always said the money was for their retirement, him and Mom. I kept telling him he had to spend money to make money. He just laughed, said he'd made a fortune on other people's money and wasn't going to start spending his own."

"And now the money is yours?"

"No, no. But it might as well be." He looked out over the ocean, and Anna thought she saw a hint of a smile pass quickly over his face. "It'll all go to Mother, of course. But she doesn't care what I do with the business. I'll be the one calling the shots."

They'd walked the full mile along the beach back to Ocean Street. She nodded to Ralph as she turned up toward Climbing Rose Cottage, expecting to part ways, but Ralph stayed by her side.

"Thank you for talking to me about this. It felt really good."

"I'm glad," Anna replied, once again surprised by Ralph's eagerness to talk to her.

"I probably sound harsh, talking about Dad like that. But I loved him. I still love him. It feels good talking about him, even if I'm complaining about him. Like I said, if you're trying to find out more about why he died, I'd love to help. Anytime."

"I appreciate that, thanks. Um, I'm going this way. I'll see you soon?" Anna gestured vaguely toward her house.

"Right. Sure. I just wanted to let you know that I'm not staying in town. Not like Mother." Ralph rolled his eyes. "She needs the pampering, I know. I'm back in Stone Harbor. But my warehouse is in Cape May Courthouse, so I'm easy to reach, and I can come down anytime."

"Okay, thanks." Anna waved as she backed away then turned and walked briskly up Columbia Avenue.

Even as she put distance between them, she could hear Ralph's voice continuing. "Anytime. Just call me. I'm sure there's more we can talk about."

"**P**hew!" Anna blew out a breath as she leaned back against the closed door of Climbing Rose Cottage. "My goodness, that man can talk."

The only response to her observation was a meow from Tough Cookie as she came in from the lounge.

"Hello?" Anna called out.

"In here." Luke's voice carried from the lounge.

Anna scooped Tough Cookie up and followed the sound. "Hey, I—" She cut herself off when she saw Patrolman Evan Burley standing in the lounge with Luke. "Oh. Hi."

"Who were you just talking about?" Luke came over and pecked Anna on the cheek.

She blushed and stepped away from Luke, dropping down onto the sofa. "Ralph Longhurst, James's son."

"The son of the man who died at White Pine Winery?" Evan asked sternly. "Why am I not surprised? Please tell me you're not getting involved in another investigation."

Anna shrugged and hid her face in Tough Cookie's fur. "Maybe. Angela doesn't think it was an accidental death."

"No, I don't suppose she would," Evan said. "No one wants to feel responsible for causing another person's death."

"All right, I'm outta here." Luke put a gentle hand on Anna's shoulder as he passed her on his way out. "I'll call you later, right?"

"Absolutely." Anna smiled at him.

Evan moved across the room, following Luke's footsteps, but glanced at Anna as he passed. He paused at the mantel, picking up the large conch shell she kept there and turning it over in his hands.

"What?" Anna finally asked. "What's bugging you?"

Evan shrugged and replaced the shell. "Nothing. Really. I came over to see you but got to talking with Luke."

"Huh. I guess that's good. You two should be friends." She meant what she said but couldn't help feeling uncomfortable at the idea of the two men talking alone with each other. *Why on earth does that bother me?* she wondered.

"Luke mentioned what happened the other day," Evan said.

"Oh. That. It was just dinner."

"What?" Evan lowered his brows in confusion.

"Wait, what? What are you talking about?"

"The call from your professor. Encouraging you to go back to school."

"Oh. That. Right." Anna jumped up from the sofa and walked to the far side of the room from Evan. She straightened up an already perfectly straight bookcase as she responded without looking at him. "Yeah, I'm not really thinking about that."

"Why not?" Evan crossed the room toward her. "I know you miss your research. I can tell just by the way you talk about it."

"You can?" Anna felt a flush of pride. "But what about Climbing Rose Cottage? I can't abandon it now."

"Of course not. I'm sure you could do both. Hire a manager to take care of the day-to-day business, or hire a cleaning service. That's most of your workload right there." Evan stood directly behind her. She could smell the fresh pine of his aftershave, or maybe it was his soap.

She took a step sideways before turning around. "That's true. But..."

"Look, I'm not trying to push you into anything. You should do what you want. It's just that I have a feeling you might want to finish your dissertation. You said you're so close. What did you call it, All But Dissertation?"

Anna laughed. "ABD, that's right. I'm impressed you remembered that."

Evan looked surprised. "I remember everything you tell me, Anna. About Mexico and Philadelphia and how you did your research."

"Oh." Anna giggled to cover her embarrassment. "Do you really think I should restart my work? It's almost as if you're pushing me away."

"Never!" Evan put his hands on Anna's arms and looked down into her eyes. "Just because I think you should follow your dreams doesn't mean I want you to leave Cape May, or even spend less time here."

Anna blinked into his deep-brown eyes, wondering why she had never noticed his long lashes before. Or the strength in his arms as he gave her one last squeeze before letting go.

"I don't want you to leave, Anna. I just want you to be happy and do what you want to do."

Anna realized she'd been staring into his eyes for a little too long. She cleared her throat and forced herself to focus on the mantel across the room. "Right. Thanks. I... uh... I need to go get Eoin."

A slight smile cut across Evan's face as he watched her then faded as fast as it had come. "Give the kid my best, will you?" He winked back at her as he strolled out of the room.

Anna released the breath she'd been holding.

13

"**C**ousin Anna, Cousin Anna, look what I made!" Eoin came running over as soon as Anna stepped into Felicia and Kathy's house, waving a blank piece of paper.

Anna swept Eoin into a big hug, but he wriggled free and held the paper up again.

"Okay, okay, what am I looking at? It looks like a blank piece of paper."

"Exactly." Eoin winked. At least she thought it was a wink. The small boy's eyes were so big behind his round glasses it looked more like a wonky blink.

"Anna, come in." Felicia trotted out to the front hall from the kitchen at the back, her bright eyes twinkling in her deeply tanned face. She pushed a hand through her short gray hair, and a few strands stayed pulled back for a moment before falling into place. "Eoin, give her a chance."

Anna gave her friend a quick hug and let her lead the way to the kitchen, shaking her head. "That boy's certainly a handful, Anna. I'll give you that."

"All right, what have you all been up to while I was out?" Anna surveyed the layout in the kitchen.

Bowls of lemon juice and a pile of cotton swabs covered the kitchen counter along with a few sheets of damp white paper wrinkled up and piled in a corner. On the table, black construction paper lay next to a bowl of white powder. Blobs of white, presumably from the powder, painted an odd pattern on several pieces of construction paper, but a few looked a little more intentional. Those were neatly taped up with packing tape. Thoroughly confused, Anna waved hello to Kathy, who stood at a counter across the room.

"Thank you again for watching Eoin while I was running my errands this morning." Anna ran her hands over the bizarre collection of items. "What on earth have you been doing?"

"Just having some fun," Felicia replied.

"Fun with science." Eoin's head bobbed excitedly up and down.

"You know I love having the boy around." Felicia beamed down at Eoin, who beamed right back up at her. "We've already fed him his lunch, though knowing him, he'll probably be hungry again in an hour."

"Why don't we sit out back and have a cold drink?" Kathy piled a pitcher and glasses onto a tray.

"Wait, wait, I need to show you." Eoin waved his blank paper frantically at Anna.

"Okay, okay. Let me do it." Felicia laughed as she took the paper from Eoin. She lit a gas ring on the stove then held the paper up high enough to keep it out of the flames as it heated up. As Anna watched, writing slowly appeared on the previously blank paper.

"A secret message!" Anna cried. "I love it."

Eoin looked like he would burst with excitement at any moment. "And there's more!"

He ran to the table, shuffled through the construction paper, then selected one piece. He carried it carefully over to Anna, balanced on his hands with the top surface flat. "Look."

Anna looked down at the paper he held. A small white fingerprint showed clearly in the center of the page, covered in clear tape.

"It's my fingerprint," Eoin explained. "I wet my finger, then I dipped it in the powder, then Felicia helped me put it on the paper, then we had to tape it to keep it safe."

"He's a fast learner," Felicia added. "Just a few tries before he was doing it all perfectly."

"I'm impressed," Anna said with feeling. "You've done so much today. Secret messages, collecting fingerprints. You're going to be a spy or a detective one day, aren't you?"

Eoin nodded eagerly. "Just like Patrolman Evan, right?"

"Come on, you two." Kathy paused in the doorway, carrying the tray of lemonade while holding the screen door open with her foot. "Let's move this outside."

Anna jumped to grab the door for her while Eoin focused on carrying his fingerprint safely.

Anna loved sitting out in Felicia's tiny but beautiful yard. Carefully trimmed mountain laurel lined two sides of it, creating a natural barrier, while a weathered-wood fence bordered the third side. A brick-paved patio provided a hard surface for the round, wrought iron table and chairs on which they sat. Bird feeders hung from trees and posts, while butterflies flitted around the flowering delphinium. The sounds of the town, never too loud to begin with, were completely silenced in the natural retreat.

While Eoin squatted on the pavement with the bowl of lemon juice and a fresh piece of paper to compose another secret message, Anna, Kathy, and Felicia settled around the small garden table with their lemonade.

"I hear you're involved in another murder investigation." Felicia took a sip.

Anna laughed. "Word travels fast. I haven't even been able to prove that it was murder yet."

"If it wasn't murder, then why are you investigating?"

Anna shrugged. "Because Angela asked me to. She's so upset. Did you hear that she's selling the winery?"

"Oh no." Kathy sighed.

"That's terrible," Felicia agreed. "We hadn't heard. Though I do know some people who won't be too upset."

"What do you mean? Who could possibly see any good in this?"

Felicia raised an eyebrow as she glanced at Kathy. Kathy shook her head in warning, but Felicia continued anyway. "I heard through the grapevine that Dean Harrison was hanging around White Pine Winery just the other morning."

"Who's Dean Harrison?" Anna glanced back and forth between Kathy and Felicia, waiting for someone to enlighten her.

"Dean runs a different winery, dear, not far away."

"So why wouldn't he be at White Pine Winery? I assume all the local winemakers are friends," Anna said.

"Hah!" Kathy barked out a laugh. "Hardly."

"Dean's never been a fan of White Pine Winery," Felicia explained. "Not since Angela took it over, anyway."

"Why not?"

Felicia offered a slight shrug. "If you ask me, he feels threatened by it."

"He gave a presentation at my club about local produce," Kathy added. "I hadn't thought of wine as local produce before, but of course it's the grapes, isn't it? Very informative. He's a strong proponent of keeping the traditional New Jersey wines going strong."

"But I don't understand," Anna pressed. "Why would he be threatened by Angela's winery?"

"It's like Kathy said," Felicia explained. "Dean makes traditional New Jersey wines. Some are fruity. Most are fairly sweet. Angela was mixing things up, testing out new grapes for this area, new blends."

Anna laughed. "Are you suggesting he might have been trying to take out the competition? That's a pretty tough way of doing it!"

"Of course not." Felicia waved away the suggestion. "It just struck me as odd that he would have been there."

Anna paused. "What day did you say he was there?"

"Let me see." Felicia put a finger on her lip then blinked and shook her head. "Oh, of course, Michelle said she saw him on Monday morning."

"Dean was there the morning of James's death. That's interesting."

"Don't go jumping to conclusions," Kathy warned. "First of all, you only have one person saying she may have seen Dean at the winery. And even if he was there, you still don't know that James was intentionally killed."

"I know. You're right. I just don't believe for a second that Angela was so careless with her winery." Anna chewed on her lip as she thought. "I don't know where to focus. Too many things are going on, too many choices."

"Like what, dear?"

"Well, for starters, was James even the intended victim?" Anna asked.

Both women inhaled sharply.

"What do you mean?" Kathy asked.

Anna shrugged. "Just that... well, if Angela's equipment was tampered with, we can't be sure that the person who did it knew that James would be the next person in there. What if they weren't trying to kill him?"

"You mean someone might have been trying to kill Angela?" Felicia put her glass down and leaned forward, a frown creasing her forehead. "Who would do that?"

"I don't know, I really don't. And it's just a thought, not..." She grinned to herself as she thought of what Luke would say. "Not evidence."

"But James is the one who died," Kathy pointed out. "Aren't you thinking about who might want to kill him?"

"I am," Anna replied. "Isabelle Longhurst, James's widow, for a start. And I can't ignore his son, Ralph, either."

"Natural suspects." Felicia nodded.

"If he was actually murdered," Kathy added.

"Who benefits?" Felicia asked.

"From James's death? Both Isabelle and Ralph, as far as I can tell," Anna said.

"And what about from the winery closing?" Felicia asked.

"We don't know it's closing," Anna pointed out. "It won't be Angela's anymore, but someone else could keep it running."

"Completely revamped under new ownership, that sort of thing?" Felicia asked.

"Sure, why not?" Kathy agreed. "Seems likely to me that whoever buys it would want to keep the business."

"So it might just be that someone wanted Angela out of business." Anna seriously considered that idea. "Maybe they weren't trying to kill someone at all. They just thought they could do enough damage that Angela would end up selling."

"And instead someone died." Kathy shook her head. "That would be truly tragic."

"And it brings us back to Dean Harrison," Felicia added.

Anna almost choked on her lemonade as she saw the excitement in Felicia's eyes. "I still think that's an extreme way to beat out the competition. That can't be a motive."

"But it's worth looking into."

"I guess. How many other wineries are in the area, though? That's a lot to look into."

"But Dean is the only one who we know didn't like White Pine Winery and who was there that morning. And as Kathy said, he's made it very clear how much he values the traditional way of doing things. He doesn't like to shake things up."

"Well, I would say murder is certainly shaking things up," Anna pointed out as she finished her lemonade. She glanced at her watch. "I think I need to call Luke."

14

"When you suggested visiting a winery for our second date, I admit I assumed you meant one that was still open." Luke parked his truck in Angela's gravel lot.

"Sorry about that." Anna wrinkled her nose. "I wasn't sure how willing you'd be to help me out with this."

He paused in the act of stepping out of the truck to look back at her. "I told you before, anything you need, you just ask. I'm here for you."

Anna felt herself blush for not having been honest with Luke. "You did, and I'm sorry. Thank you for coming here with me."

As they approached the winery door—the Closed sign big and red in the middle of the door—it swung open with a bang. The man who burst through it stood a few inches taller than Luke, lean but muscular arms showing off a tan that came from working outside rather than lying in the sun. He carried a box overflowing with what looked like CDs, books, clothes, and other odds and ends piled into a haphazard bunch.

He paused when he saw Anna and Luke. His eyes skimmed over Anna, and he nodded a greeting to Luke before sliding the box into the back of an old Mustang.

Luke grabbed the door before it swung shut again and ushered Anna inside, the Mustang's tires squealing on the gravel as it pulled away. Inside, the winery looked the same as Anna remembered, but everything seemed stiller, quieter.

Angela once again stood behind the tall counter, but today her normally silky hair hung ragged and loose around her shoulders. She wiped a hand ungracefully across her nose as she looked up at them, her eyes red from crying. "At least Rick is happy." She sniffled.

"Rick?" Anna asked, surprised by the comment.

"My ex-boyfriend, Rick Enright. He hated how much time I spent at this place. That's what finally drove us apart."

"Is that who we just saw leaving?"

Luke nodded. "That was Rick. He works in town. A mechanic."

"I'm so sorry, Angela. First breaking up with your boyfriend, now losing the winery. It's all too much, isn't it?" Anna stepped behind the counter to hug her friend.

Angela sniffled again and nodded. "It's just not fair."

"I know how much time it takes to run your own business," Anna added.

"And you like to throw in a little crime solving too." Luke raised an eyebrow at Anna.

Anna gave him a look that she hoped told him to knock it off. To Angela, she said, "If it makes you feel any better, he didn't look too happy either."

Angela sniffled again and straightened up. "Thank you. Maybe that does make me feel better. I still can't believe how angry he got. He never used to be like that.

When we first started dating, he loved that I owned this place."

"Maybe he just didn't understand how much time you would need to put into running the winery."

"He didn't," Angela agreed. "I tried to explain it to him. He said he always felt like he came second in our relationship—after the winery."

Luke shrugged. "I can understand why he would feel like that. You have something you love that takes a lot of your time. If he didn't have a similar job, it would be hard for him to relate to."

"But that's no reason to take it out on Angela." Anna raised her eyebrows at Luke then turned her attention back to Angela as an idea crossed her mind. "He wouldn't try to sabotage your winery, would he?"

Angela scoffed. "Of course not. Definitely not. We only broke up last week. Like I said, he was just jealous, saying that I cared more about the vineyard than about him."

"So..." Luke looked around the shop. "We came to look at your mechanics, right?"

"That's right," Anna agreed. "I'm sorry to drag you through this again, Angela, but can you show us the tank room so Luke can take a look around?"

Angela looked back and forth between them, clearly surprised by the request, but nodded. As they followed her, Anna once again took in the details of the large barn that opened off the back of the public shop, the doorway to her left showing off the patio area and a glimpse of vines.

In the tank room, Angela pointed out a panel hidden in the wall. Half the height of a door, the panel was painted the same color as the wall, unobtrusive and easily missed. "That's where the police focused their attention."

Luke pulled the panel down and poked around through the mechanics it hid. "Well, here you go." He grunted as he backed out of the tight space, pointing at a series of cables linked to a vent. "Ventilation systems like this use a vent damper to draw in outside air. But it's easy for the linkage on the damper to seize up or break. I have to check these things on any building I'm working on."

"And this one is broken?" Anna asked.

"You could say that." Luke nodded. "It's stuck in the closed position."

"So no fresh air is coming in to circulate?" Anna asked.

"And in this room, that's dangerous," Angela added.

Luke pointed at the tangle of cables. "You can see where the line's worn through."

"Worn? Or cut?" Anna asked.

"Good question. It could be wear and tear. It's a little ragged here." Luke used his boot to shift the cable slightly, examining it closely. "No, that doesn't look like natural wearing or even chewing to me. It's been sawed through with something not quite sharp enough. This was no accident." He looked over at Anna. "If the police were looking through here, that means they already noticed this. I'm sure they took fingerprints, DNA, whatever they do." He replaced the panel in the wall and wiped his hands off on his jeans. "I don't think there's anything you can add to this, Anna. You're going to need to let them do their job."

"Right." Anna voiced agreement but kept other thoughts to herself. She took Angela by the arm as they walked back to the main store. "Come on, we'll help you pack up. But, Angela?"

Angela looked over at her. "Yes?"

"I'm not giving up on this. Based on what Luke just found, it really was murder. And that means you didn't kill James. I'm still going to try fixing this so you can reopen the winery."

Angela leaned into a hug as she let out a long sigh.

"Thank you, Anna. I can't tell you what it means to have you on my side."

Anna glanced back at Luke, who had stopped to grab a stack of empty boxes and carry them over to the counter. No matter what Luke might think, Anna could definitely do more here—including looking into Rick Enright. She pulled out her phone and sent a quick text then tucked the phone away before Luke saw it. It probably wasn't a good sign that she was keeping secrets from him after only one real date, but there was no reason he needed to know she was ignoring his advice, and she certainly didn't want to argue about it.

❧ 15 ❧

Anna sat on her front porch steps waiting, running her hands through Tough Cookie's fur, enjoying the sounds of the cat's satisfied purrs. As soon as Evan pushed through the front gate, she sprang up and ran to him. Tough Cookie let out an insulted meow and jumped down into the flower bed.

"Thank you for coming. I appreciate it."

"No problem." Evan laughed as he gave her a quick peck on the cheek. "What can I do to help?"

"I have a few questions—and a few ideas I'd like to run by you."

"Questions about what?" Evan settled down onto the porch where Anna had just been sitting.

She plopped down next to him. "The murder." She felt Evan stiffen next to her.

"The murder?"

She nodded. "Angela's struggling. You know she's going to have to sell her winery? It's terrible!"

"I really am sorry to hear that." Evan sounded like he meant it.

Anna leaned closer to him. "Thank you. I know you are. Evan, I went to the winery. I saw that her ventilation thing was stuck closed. Luke said he could tell the line had been cut. That suggests someone did this, doesn't it? I want to help. I know I can help."

Evan shook his head and laughed again. "You're unstoppable, aren't you?"

Anna raised one eyebrow as she shrugged in response, relieved that Evan had relaxed.

"All right, listen, this isn't public information yet, but you're right. Not only was the linkage cut to keep the vent closed, James's oxygen meter was intentionally tampered with too."

"I knew it!" Anna pumped her arm in victory then stopped. "Oh, sorry. That's not actually good news, is it?"

Evan gave her a sideways look. "Not usually, no. Look, don't get so excited. Our official position is still that the most likely cause was negligence."

Anna raised one eyebrow again. "Seriously? That's an awful lot of coincidence. Her air flow system somehow gets cut, and at the same time, an oxygen meter coincidentally stops working? What are the chances?"

Evan made a face Anna couldn't interpret. "It is kind of unbelievable. I know. But it's a good theory for a police department where half the staff is off helping with the manhunt."

"The manhunt? Oh, you mean the shooter from Trenton."

Evan nodded. "Even Detective Walsh is willing to accept a lot of coincidences if it means he doesn't have to look into this too much, not while we're so understaffed."

"How could the police ignore something so obvious just because of staffing problems?"

Evan took a breath. He looked down into the flower

bed, apparently enthralled by the sight of Tough Cookie stalking some unfortunate animal. Finally, he looked back at Anna. "I know. You're right."

"I am?" Her eyes opened wide in surprise.

"I'm not giving up on this."

"So have you talked to the ex-boyfriend?"

Evan looked confused. "Rick Enright? No, why?"

Anna shook her head and let out an impatient sigh. "Because he has a motive. They just broke up. He was mad at her for spending so much time at the winery. I guess he felt like she wasn't paying enough attention to him." She frowned and looked down at her hands. "I know the type."

Evan stared at her for a moment. "I'm sure you do. But what are you saying? Why would Rick want to kill James Longhurst?"

Anna shook her head. "He wouldn't, but maybe he wanted to get Angela's winery shut down. Maybe he didn't even intend for anyone to die. He just tampered with some of her equipment so it would fail. I don't know." Anna waved a hand. "Maybe he wanted to get her closed for a while so they could rekindle their romance. Or maybe he just wanted to get back at her because he was angry."

Evan laughed. "Why do you always find the most complicated motives? The widow is the most likely suspect. The spouse always is. She inherits everything."

"Hmm." Anna pictured Isabelle, relaxing in luxury just a few blocks away. "She was a little weird. That's true. Not entirely cut up about her husband's death."

"You already talked to James's widow?" Evan stiffened again.

"Oops." Anna wrinkled her nose in regret. "Sorry. Yes. Like I said, Angela asked me to help."

"Of course she did. You're the local Miss Marple now, aren't you?"

Anna laughed. "I don't want to be! But I guess people think I'm good at this."

Evan paused, looking her carefully in the eye. "You are good at this. I don't know why, but you're good at looking at the details, at seeing how things fit together."

Anna felt herself blush. "Thank you."

"But." Evan held up a finger. "I still think Isabelle is the most obvious suspect. And if not her, then the person who was with James at the time."

"Wait, he wasn't alone?"

Evan shook his head. "Corey Bowman, a friend of his, was at the winery too. He claims he left at the same time James wandered back into the tank room. But because they left the tasting room together, no one else can verify that. All we know for sure is that James and Corey left the tasting room. When Angela's staff found James, Corey was gone."

"Huh. Well, that is suspicious. Who is this guy?"

"Just a friend of James Longhurst—an old friend, apparently. He was at the winery to join in the celebration."

"Angela didn't tell me other people were there."

"No? That's a little odd, particularly since she asked you for help."

"It is." Anna thought back through everything Angela had told her, had shown her. "I don't know. She could've had a good reason. Maybe she didn't realize it was important. Maybe she's sure Corey's not involved."

"Maybe. But she thinks her ex-boyfriend is?"

Anna shook her head. "I don't know what she thinks. *I* think Rick was involved. You should look into him a bit. I really think so."

"Cousin Anna!" Eoin ran toward her from the back of the house. "Hurry up. It's time for tea."

"Sorry, I'll let you get back to work." Evan dusted off his

uniform pants as he stood. "And by that, I mean serving tea, not solving murders, right?"

Anna grinned. "For now, sure. But then I need to talk to Corey Bowman."

16

Corey Bowman lived in a cottage in West Cape May, in a neighborhood not far from Luke's house geographically but a world away in terms of style and character. Like many Jersey Shore towns, West Cape May was dealing with an influx of wealthy newcomers who wanted a house near the beach but weren't interested in the small cottages available. As older residents died or moved out, new owners would buy the property, its only appeal for them the land the house stood on. One by one, older houses were being torn down, replaced by mini-mansions.

Corey's street, one block up from Sunset Boulevard, seemed to have been caught in the middle of the process of gentrification. Some houses spread out across their lots, wings and porches and daintily decorated patios covering all available ground, while upper stories reached into the treetops. Corey, on the other hand, lived in what looked like one of the original houses: small, square, squat. His house had two stories, but with its sharply pitched roof, the second-floor rooms would have limited standing space.

Its size notwithstanding, the house and garden were

lovingly maintained. As Anna led Sammy and Eoin up the path to the front door, she took in the lilies, geraniums, and zinnia blooming in small beds dotting the front lawn. It wasn't perfect—a few weeds peeked up here and there, and even Anna could tell that several plants were overdue for deadheading—but the imperfections simply highlighted the tender care behind the garden. Whoever lived there took care of it. They didn't use a professional, even though they clearly weren't experts. It was a labor of love, not for show. Anna skipped up the two steps to the front door and knocked, Sammy and Eoin right behind her.

"You sure he said tonight?" Sammy asked, her voice low as she glanced around.

"I am." Anna glanced at her. "When I called earlier to introduce myself, he invited us all over tonight. Thanks for coming. I hope everything was okay at the bakery yesterday."

Sammy took a deep breath. "Kind of."

"Kind of?" Anna was going to ask more, but she spun back toward the door as she heard the bolt slide on the other side.

Anna struggled to judge the age of the man who opened the door and welcomed them into his home. He looked easily in his seventies, but she'd been told he was old friends with James, who was a decade younger. Corey's grayish skin sagged around his neck and jowls. White hair covered his scalp sporadically, long strands intertwining over bald spots. His hands, covered in dark spots, shook as he directed them through to the living room.

The inside of the house showed an equally high level of care as the exterior. Old but well-made furniture had been laid out in a sparse but elegant style. The rooms themselves felt bright and airy, despite the low ceilings. A few pieces of carefully curated artwork hung on the walls, adding to the conversation of the room rather than dominating it. Anna was no judge, but they looked like quality artwork to her. Remnants of a better time, perhaps.

Anna, Sammy, and Eoin waited in the small front room while Corey went back to the kitchen to prepare tea and cakes. When he returned carrying a tray of tea things with a plate of cookies, Eoin's face lit up, and he grabbed two.

Once they'd settled in with their tea and all the introductions had been made, Anna broached the question of Corey's participation in James's celebratory gathering at the winery.

"Yes, I was there on Monday." Corey picked up a shortbread cookie but didn't eat it. "I met James at the winery earlier, actually. We had some... business to talk about."

"Business? Did you two work together?" Anna asked.

"Oh no, nothing like that. I've been working on getting business from a winery that James knows well. He worked with them frequently. I thought he could help."

Anna glanced at Sammy, but Sammy simply smiled and took a sip of tea, so Anna continued with her questions. "How long had you known James?"

"Oh, forever. That sounds implausible, but we've been friends since childhood."

Anna looked at Sammy again. "We can relate to that, Mr. Bowman. Some people are fortunate enough to stay friends."

"Fortunate?" Sammy raised an eyebrow. "Or unfortunate?"

Anna laughed and playfully swatted a hand at Sammy.

"D'you think BethAnne and I will still be friends years from now?" Eoin asked—referring to a local high school student who had captured his fancy—his mouth full of shortbread.

"Who knows?" Anna leaned toward Eoin to tuck a

napkin into the top of his shirt. She hoped he wasn't spreading too many crumbs around the pristine room. "It's possible."

"We grew up in Stone Harbor," Corey explained. "James still lived there. Our lives have taken different turns, obviously."

"This is an adorable house, so much more character than some of these new mansions going up," Sammy observed as her gaze moved about the room.

"Thank you for saying so. I do love this house."

"It shows," Anna agreed.

"I bought this intending to rent it out, you know. Back before…"

Anna and Sammy waited, uncomfortably letting the phrase hang, not willing to push Corey for personal information he wasn't willing to share.

Eoin did not have that problem. "Before what?" he piped up.

"Ah." Corey laughed awkwardly. "Yes. I got sick, you see. Medical bills. It all worked out." He waved a hand to cut off their words of condolence. "I'm better now—mostly. But it set me back quite a bit. Lots of expenses, you know, and I couldn't work for several years. I was fortunate, really. I had some money from my parents that I used to pay the bills— hospital, medicine, home care, more medicine. Once it was done, I still had this house but no more savings. Better off than many people still, right? I went back to work and saved enough that I was able to retire… eventually."

"I'm impressed by your attitude," Anna said. "And what, exactly, is your business?"

"Wine, of course. I was in the distribution business."

"Like Ralph?"

"Correct. That young man will go far. So much energy, dedication. Very impressive. I can't claim to have been as successful as he is, but I did all right. I kept my expenses low, profits high. The best way to work."

"And you stayed in touch with the Longhursts?" Sammy reached for another cookie.

Anna raised an eyebrow at her, but Sammy just smirked. Sammy had been blessed with a metabolism that let her eat as much as she wanted without putting on weight—and she knew perfectly well Anna had not.

"Oh yes, they were very good to me. James in particular, dropping by when I was sick, keeping my spirits up. A good friend."

"And you were with him to celebrate his new contract that day?" Anna asked.

Corey nodded and frowned. "I was there. I wish I had stayed."

"I understand you left when James went into the tank room?"

"That's right. I told him I was heading home, and he said he'd walk me out, but then he got this idea in his head." He laughed softly. "That was just like him. If he wanted something, he did it."

"But you didn't go with him into the tank room?" Anna pressed the point, not sure what she was hoping to hear but curious why Corey hadn't stayed.

Corey shook his head. "I did not. I simply headed out the back door—my car was parked around back. He went right. I went left. And that was the last time I saw him." Tears welled in his eyes. "He was a good friend, and I'll miss him." Suddenly he grinned, a wicked look in his watery eyes. "But we had our moments."

"Moments?" Sammy gave a nervous laugh.

"Oh sure, you know how boys can be." He winked at Eoin.

Eoin chewed back at him.

"Like what?" Anna asked. "Anything bad?"

"Bad? As in illegal? Oh no, nothing like that. Just messing around with each other. You know how it is. Like the time he set me up to take the fall when he cheated on our French exam. Or when he convinced Margaret Trouman I was the one who'd poisoned her dog." His eyes narrowed at the memory.

"You killed someone's dog?" Sammy asked, surprised.

Even Eoin stopped chewing, his eyes focused on Corey.

"Oh no, no." Corey laughed. "The dog must have eaten something bad. It was throwing up for days, apparently. But it had nothing to do with me, I assure you." His smile dropped, and he stared out the window for a moment. "I really liked Margaret, you know. She never talked to me again." His eyes narrowed once more. "I could have killed James for doing that." He blinked and shook his head. "Now, what else can I help you with?"

17

"Point number one, he was there when James was killed." Sammy raised a finger from the steering wheel as she listed the point, and Anna could hear Eoin's pencil scratching as he wrote it down carefully in his notebook.

"Right, that's a good point one," Anna agreed.

"Point two, they may have been friends, but they clearly had a competitive relationship," Sammy said.

"That was just a story about a girl. It didn't necessarily mean anything. Although... that look in his eyes." Anna pictured the old man, still visibly angry over a lie that must have been told almost fifty years ago.

"And," Sammy continued, "he was trying to get James to help him close the deal with that other winery. I sensed some competition in that story as well."

"Right, like why would Corey have to convince James to help him? They weren't competing against each other for the winery's business."

"Just competing against each other for who was more successful. And James was definitely winning."

"That depends on what you consider success," Anna pointed out. "James had money, clearly, but hardly a happy family life."

"Corey doesn't seem to have any family life at all."

"But he's happy to be alive. He's clearly grateful for what he has."

"He knows the machinery involved," Sammy continued. "He could have cut that line, tampered with the oxygen meter."

"True."

Anna thought about what it all meant as Eoin scribbled away. Then the sound of writing stopped.

"Cousin Anna?"

"Yes, honey?"

"What d'you mean when you say a happy family life? Is that the same as having a happy family?"

"I suppose it is." Anna turned in her seat to look back at Eoin. "It just means that when a family lives together—like you and me—we love each other, and we take care of each other."

"We watch out for each other." Eoin nodded his agreement, beaming at her.

"Exactly."

Anna turned to face forward, watching the tourists as Sammy drove slowly through the crowded town. Eoin yawned loudly from the back seat, and Anna felt guilt rise at keeping him out after eight. Sunset Boulevard turned into Clifton Street, and the pedestrian traffic picked up. People darted across the street, running from one antique store to another, popping into the tea shop then back to the antique stores. As they made the turn toward Washington Mall, they slowed even more.

Sammy chose to take Beach Avenue to avoid the busiest crowds, but it didn't help. Even at night, cars had to crawl along to avoid pedestrians dashing across the road to view the ocean at night or stepping out into the street to make room on the sidewalk. Lights from the stores lit up one side of the street while the ocean lay dark and ominous on the other. Only a few stars lit the path for a bold few venturing out onto the dark beach.

Anna turned to watch her friend in profile. She looked as beautiful as always, but something was bothering her. "Sammy, is something going on at the bakery?"

"You could say that. I'm just not sure what."

"Tell me," Anna urged her.

"Things have gone missing. Little things." Sammy waved a hand dismissively. "At first I thought they were just getting misplaced. But it's become too common. And yesterday..." Her voice trailed off as she shook her head.

"What happened yesterday?"

"Yesterday, it was cash."

Anna inhaled sharply but didn't say anything.

"At least I assume that was what happened. Mark came up short when he was closing up. I don't know." Sammy shrugged one shoulder.

"Have you called the police?"

Sammy gave Anna a sideways glance. "About a missing mixing bowl? A stolen spatula? Of course not."

"But now that it's cash..."

Sammy nodded. "That changes things. I'll need to keep a closer eye on my staff. I need to figure out who's stealing from me."

"You really think it's one of your employees? Can I help?"

"No, you've got enough on your plate. Clearly. Speaking of which"—Sammy raised an eyebrow—"Corey and James were friends, but Corey admitted they'd fought too."

Anna opened her mouth to ask more about the thefts at

the bakery but realized Sammy had intentionally changed the topic. When she wanted Anna's help, she would ask. Anna turned her attention back to Corey Bowman instead and his childhood arguments with James Longhurst. "Enough to kill?" she asked skeptically.

"Hmm, I guess not." Sammy pursed her lips as she thought. "Well, I mean, we've been friends forever, and we would never hurt each other..."

"But he's not us." Anna finished Sammy's thought.

"Exactly. Ha! I still remember that time you convinced my mom I had to do all that extra homework."

"Only to get you back for making it sound like I was snoring in class!"

They were still laughing and reminiscing when Sammy pulled into the small parking area behind Climbing Rose Cottage. Anna had pulled her seat belt off and opened the door before she realized no sounds were coming from the back seat.

She opened the back door as quietly as she could, but Eoin stirred and rubbed his eyes. "Are we home?"

"We are. Do you want me to carry you in?"

Sammy gave Anna a skeptical look from the driver's seat, and fortunately, Eoin rejected the offer. It was unlikely she would have been able to carry him far.

"I'm not a baby." He gave another big yawn as he toppled out of the car.

Anna kept a hand on Eoin's shoulder as they made their way inside, then she followed him upstairs, helped him get washed up, and tucked him in bed.

She ran her hand through his curly mop of red hair and kissed his forehead. "I love you, Eoin."

"I love you, too, Cousin An..." His words trailed off as his eyes closed.

Anna felt tears in her eyes. *How could this small boy have touched my heart so deeply in such a short time?* She leaned over and softly kissed his forehead once more, then tiptoed to his door and silently let herself out.

She was still smiling broadly as she descended the stairs, but her gentle mood was disturbed by the doorbell ringing. Wondering who would be showing up that late, Anna pulled the door open then gasped. "Oh no, I forgot!"

Her mother stood on the porch, and she did not look happy.

$\mathscr{S}$ 18 $\mathscr{S}$

"I really am sorry, Mom." Anna couldn't stop apologizing, even as she pulled together the ingredients she needed for the lemon poppyseed muffins she was serving that morning.

"I told you, don't worry about it." Barbara McGregor leaned casually against the kitchen counter, rubbing an apple with a clean dishcloth. She wore exercise capris splashed with bright splotches of pink, green, and yellow topped with a loose bright-yellow tank top of the moisture-wicking variety. With her strawberry-blond hair pulled up into a high ponytail, she could easily pass for a woman half her age. From a distance, anyway.

Anna shook her head and reached for a mixing bowl. "I was sure I gave you the code to get in. I still don't understand why you didn't call me."

Barbara shrugged. "Like I told you last night, I was fine. You know I still have friends in town. I took the opportunity to spend some time with them. I haven't had a girls' night out in ages—it was fabulous." She took a bite of the apple.

They hadn't talked much the night before. Anna had been exhausted from a long day, and her mother had been a little worse for wear from her night out. Anna had mostly just apologized repeatedly for not being there when her mother arrived while getting her settled into her room.

"Now, when are we going to have our talk?" Barbara looked around the kitchen. "Probably not right now."

Anna looked over her kitchen and could imagine what her mother was thinking. Making and serving breakfast for ten guests wasn't easy, but Anna had worked out a system. It involved spreading a variety of plates and bowls of ingredients in strategic places around the kitchen. To her, it made perfect sense. To her mother, it probably looked like a disaster.

"I'm sorry, this tends to be the busiest time of day for me."

Barbara held up a hand. "Stop apologizing, and don't worry. I could use some exercise this morning. We can talk after I take a walk on the beach. Where's Eoin?"

Barbara looked around as if expecting the boy to be hiding under the table or behind a curtain—which, for Eoin, wouldn't be entirely out of character.

Anna smiled at the thought, and her mother looked at her quizzically. "Sorry, just thinking of something. He's out on the porch. He likes to meet the guests and tell them all about what they can do while they're in Cape May."

"That's sweet." Barbara's eyes softened. "He's really enjoyed his time here, hasn't he? I admit I'm a little surprised."

"Surprised, why?" Anna asked just as a timer went off. She grabbed a potholder and pulled a tray of baked French toast out of the oven then reached for the bowl of strawberries to wash and cut.

"Never mind." Barbara waved a hand, stood up straight,

and put on her sunglasses. "Like I said, later." She waved as she left through the back door, avoiding having to confront any guests while in her workout clothes.

Anna plated two breakfasts then carried them through the dining room and out to the porch. Just as on most beautiful mornings, all of her guests had opted to eat breakfast on the porch rather than inside. Eoin stood next to the table she was aiming for, on his toes with his arms spread wide. As Anna approached, she realized he was regaling the young couple with a story about the great blue heron.

"I recommend the state park too." She served them their breakfasts. "Eoin is not wrong about that." She smiled at them, checked on her other guests, then headed back inside, tickling Tough Cookie behind the ear as she passed.

The cat had adopted her usual breakfast position, perched on a chair in the dining room, with a clear view of the guests outside and right in Anna's path as she moved back and forth between the kitchen and her guests. "Keeping an eye on things, Tough Cookie? Everything going well?"

Tough Cookie looked up at Anna and yawned. Anna took that as a positive sign.

Back in the kitchen, she popped four pieces of bread into the toaster and reached for her laptop. No reason she shouldn't use the time to do a little research on James Longhurst. She'd heard a lot about him already but always from people with their own biases and perspectives. *Was James the good and caring friend Corey knew? Or the dedicated oenophile Ralph remembered? Or the selfish and focused man Isabelle had described? Or all of the above?*

As often turned out to be the case, social media proved to be a bonanza of information. James's profile hadn't been removed, and Anna scrolled through the photos that were available for anyone to see. She could understand why Isabelle had described James's love for wine as a fetish. Every picture he shared involved wine—James drinking it, a few bottles artfully placed, an image of wine being poured, another of a winery tank room.

The pop of the toaster brought her mind back to the present. She grabbed the toast, a small bowl of butter, jam, and a fresh carafe of coffee and headed back out to the porch, nodding at Tough Cookie on the way.

As she topped off her guests' coffee cups, she thought about what her social media posts would tell people about her. Pictures of the places she'd traveled and worked, of course. And recently, lots of pictures of Eoin, obviously. She stopped mid-pour. Pictures of Eoin, of course.

"Hello?" The woman she was serving looked up at her expectantly. "I'd like a full cup, if that's okay."

"Right, sorry." Anna laughed. "Where was my mind?" She finished serving then hurried inside.

Tough Cookie put out a paw to stop her.

"What?"

The cat blinked at her.

"I know, that's what I was just thinking. Where's his family in all this?"

She rushed back to the kitchen and leaned over her laptop. It was true. He hadn't posted a single picture of his family. From James's page, she connected to a page put up by Isabelle. It looked pretty much like Anna would have expected—a few pictures of Isabelle with a group of women her age, presumably friends, a picture of Ralph as a child as she wished him a happy birthday, even one of Isabelle with James at an elegant function.

Anna scrolled through the images, smiling at how frequently Isabelle posted pictures involving shopping—her out with friends at a store, items she'd just purchased, even a few memes about shopping therapy. Isabelle might have spent a little too much time shopping, but at least she had a sense of humor about it.

Based on the comments below some of the pictures, Ralph apparently didn't agree. One comment stood out as particularly harsh. "Don't spend it all at once!" The laughing emoji appended to the end of the text did not do enough to cut the sting from the words. Now that Isabelle had control of the Longhursts' money, she could imagine Ralph meant what he said.

Then again, the shopping hadn't started after James's death. A group of images showed off another big shopping spree, one just a few days before James died. *Could Isabelle have known she was about to gain control of all their money? Or had shopping been her way of getting back at James for paying more attention to his wine habit than to her?* Anna laughed at the absurdity of a wealthy couple driving each other crazy with their hobbies.

Her smile froze as her eyes fell on the next image. She squinted and leaned in closer. *Is that...? Could that be...?* She shook her head, thinking.

Her hands working on autopilot, she cut up a bowl of fruit, plated another serving of the French toast, and carried the tray back out to the porch. Tough Cookie meowed as she passed without acknowledging the cat, but Anna's mind was elsewhere.

Once back in the kitchen, Anna focused on the image still visible on her screen. Isabelle posed with a group of young people more than half her age, college students, from the look of it. They stood as a group in a classroom. A small, old-fashioned blackboard hung on the wall behind them, but most of the space was taken up by carts and tables covered in what looked like parts of an engine. The scene was bizarre enough, Isabelle not only spending time in a classroom but a classroom clearly dedicated to a mechanical course, but that wasn't all. The most unexpected part of the photo was the person standing off to the right of the group, looking smugly self-satisfied: Rick Enright.

❧ 19 ☙

Anna kept her eyes on the picture of Isabelle and Rick as she finished her conversation with Evan. "I knew you'd understand. Why else would Isabelle take a course from Rick Enright?"

"I don't know, but I'll definitely look into it. If this turns out to be the lead we need to break the case, even Detective Walsh will be grateful to you. You know he didn't want to bring any staff back from the manhunt."

"Will you let me know what you find? About what the course was and why Isabelle took it?"

Silence filled the other end of the line.

"Evan?"

"I'm here, I'm here. It's just… I don't know what I can tell you, but I'll definitely let you know as much as I can, okay?"

"I guess that will have to do."

Anna hung up and looked at the mess she'd let build in the kitchen. At least Evan immediately grasped how significant that photo could be. Not only did Isabelle know Rick, but she'd taken a course from him—a course that could easily have given her the know-how she needed to cut the line in Angela's tank room and tamper with the oxygen meter.

Sighing, Anna started the hot water running to fill up the sink with sudsy water, ready to tackle the stack of dishes waiting for attention.

"Anna, you in here?" Barbara's voice floated in from the lounge.

"In the kitchen, Mom," Anna called back to her.

Barbara stuck her head around the door. "Any of that yummy breakfast left? I'm starving after my walk." Barbara had showered and dressed in a flowing sundress and comfortable sandals, her hair falling in loose waves around her shoulders.

Anna had always been jealous of her mother's hair. Where Anna had a mass of curls nearly impossible to control, her mother's hair seemed to fall into naturally elegant waves that curled lightly around her face and shoulders.

"French toast?" She looked around. "Scrambled eggs?"

"Hmm, maybe something lighter? I don't want to eat all the calories I just burned off."

"How about yogurt and fresh fruit?"

"Perfect!"

"Grab a seat in the dining room, Mom. I'll bring it out to you. It's too messy to eat in here."

Barbara did what she was told, and Anna carried out a tray with yogurt, fresh-cut fruit, and coffee. In the dining room, dainty lace tablecloths covered small tables just big enough for two. Anna had placed a motley collection of era-appropriate chairs at the tables and decorated the room with lamps, pictures, and trinkets from that time. Barbara was already settled at a small table in the dining room with Eoin, chatting away.

Relieved that Eoin was there to distract her mother, Anna returned her focus to cleaning up the kitchen and then the rest of the house. She'd been up half the night worrying about why her mother was there and what her big news was, but she couldn't let that stop her from doing her job thoroughly, even when that meant scraping eggs off a plate or changing the sheets on six beds. If Barbara was there to talk her out of running that business, the best thing she could do was work even harder to avoid creating the slipshod environment her mother probably expected.

When Anna came upstairs with the empty laundry basket, ready to strip the beds, her mother was waiting for her in the front hall.

"I see you're still busy, dear."

"I'm sorry, Mom. I know we need to talk. I just need to get the sheets going in the washer, then I'm all yours."

"This is important, dear. Can't I grab a few minutes of your time?"

Anna sighed and dropped the basket, tucking it behind the basement door. "Of course, Mom. Come on. I'll have a cup of coffee with you."

Eoin had settled into his usual seat on the front porch, and from where Anna and Barbara sat in the dining room, Anna could see him alternatively nodding then frowning at whatever he was reading.

Barbara leaned back in her chair, and it let out a small creak. She leaned forward, surprised, but Anna waved a hand.

"They all make that noise sometimes. It's fine, and it's not you!"

Barbara laughed. "I'm glad to hear it. You really have done a great job fixing this old place up."

"Thank you," Anna said, surprised to get the compliment from her mother. "I've worked hard at it."

"I could see that just this morning. Are you doing this all on your own?"

"I've had some help. Do you remember Luke Arnold?"

Her mother furrowed her brow, thinking. "Arnold... Arnold... ah yes, I remember, the handyman, right? But his name's not Luke, and he must be far too old to do much around the house anymore."

"Luke is his son. He took over the business when his father retired."

"Ah." Anna's mom looked at her carefully. "And there's something else you're not telling me. Is he attractive?"

Anna felt herself blush. "He's been great doing work around the house. You saw the rooms. He had to tear some of those down to the baseboards."

"Mm-hmm." Barbara took a sip of coffee. "Nevertheless, you know there's not much of a future in running a B and B."

Anna sat back and sighed, waiting for the lecture she'd been dreading all morning.

"You've done better than I expected," Barbara continued.

"Really?" Anna leaned forward. "Thank you!"

Barbara's hands tightened around her coffee cup, but she maintained her smile. "I'm not saying this is necessarily the choice I would have made for you, but if it's what you want..." She let the words hang as a question.

"It is," Anna said firmly. Then she added, "At least I think so. For now, anyway."

Barbara nodded. "Okay then. But that wasn't actually what I wanted to talk to you about."

"It's not?"

"No." Barbara took another sip of coffee, draining her cup.

Anna jumped up and grabbed the carafe from the sideboard. She poured her mother a fresh cup and topped off her own. If she kept this up, she'd be bouncing off the walls all morning.

"It's about Eoin," Barbara said once Anna sat down again. "His parents are getting divorced."

The unexpected news hit Anna like a punch in the gut. She swallowed hard, trying to tamp down the churning in her stomach. "What happened?"

"I don't know the details. You know Eoin is related on your father's side."

Anna nodded. "Sure, Uncle Sean is Dad's cousin."

"Correct. And they're not particularly close. When Sean went off to university in Ireland, he met Eoin's mother, and they fell in love. He settled down in Ireland, but he might as well have been on Mars. He hardly ever calls. Your father and I never see them and only talk to them a couple of times a year."

"So when did you hear about the divorce?"

"Maura, Sean's soon-to-be-ex-wife, called me. She didn't share all the details, of course, but it's not amicable. That was why they were eager to pack him off to Cape May for the summer."

Anna took a sip of coffee as she thought about it then pushed the still-full cup away, her stomach doing flips. "So, what happens next? Who will take him?"

"They're still working out the terms of that. They're thinking of sending him to a boarding school. Maura travels so much for work, and apparently, Sean isn't prepared to raise Eoin on his own. Now, this is from Maura's perspective, mind you, but she said he's more committed to his retirement than raising a young boy. And frankly, that sounds like the Sean I remember."

"That's terrible!" Anna leaned back in her chair, wrapping her arms around her stomach. She felt like she was going to throw up. "Eoin's not going to like that idea at all."

Eoin, a tiny figure engulfed by the big Adirondack chair, looked up. He caught Anna's eye through the window and grinned, the sunlight glinting off his round glasses. Anna smiled sadly back.

❧ 2 0 ☙

Barbara stood then leaned down and kissed Anna on the top of her head. "I'll let you get back to your work. I have some shopping I want to do, anyway. We'll talk more when I get back, okay?"

Anna blew out a breath, wishing she could join her mother shopping, wishing she could forget what her mom had just told her. The news would devastate Eoin. She was sure of it. He was so eager to get back to school, to see his friends.

She tried to focus on her work, but her mind kept spinning with images. Eoin, tiny and lost in a new school, no parent to tuck him in at night, none of his old friends to keep him company. She felt tears building in her eyes and shook her head. "Don't be melodramatic, Anna. Children go to boarding schools all the time. They're not all like something out of a Dickens novel."

The chime of the doorbell finally forced her to focus on the present instead of the imagined future. Tucking the full laundry basket she was carrying out of sight again, Anna answered the door.

Without a word, Isabelle Longhurst swept into the house, draped in a soft white cotton scarf that hung artfully over her bare shoulders, covering the pale-pink sundress underneath. She lowered her sunglasses just enough to look briefly around the space then turned and walked into the lounge. Ralph came trotting in after her.

"I'm so sorry. I apologize for my mother. She's a woman on a mission, and well, you know." He smiled pathetically, and Anna felt a pang of pity for him.

"Of course, come in." Anna took a moment to bring her mind back to the case, trying to push images of a scared and lost Eoin away. "Would you like some coffee or tea?"

"No, thank you," Isabelle responded, even though the question had been directed at Ralph. "This won't take long." Isabelle had placed herself in the center of the lounge, not sitting but standing by the large bay window. "Ralph tells me you asked him questions about James's death too. Why?"

"Oh." Anna shook her head, barely thinking about the question. "I thought I'd explained when I met you at the Restful Retreat Inn. I'm not trying to intrude on your grief."

"Grief? Hardly," Isabelle scoffed. "But what business is it of yours?"

Ralph slid by Anna to stand next to his mother, but she ignored him.

"What business is it?" Anna felt her anger rise. This was the last thing she needed. She needed to focus on Eoin, not on a spoiled, nasty woman. "I'm a friend of Angela's. She asked me to help, so that makes it my business."

Ralph shifted his weight, looking back and forth between Anna and Isabelle. As he moved, the standing lamp next to him flickered off and on again. Anna almost growled in frustration but ignored it.

"Yes, she's a dear girl. We've known her for years." Isabelle's words were kind, but the tone didn't convey the same sentiment. She examined the ugly lamp from top to bottom then turned back to Anna. "I was very sorry to hear she has to sell the winery, but perhaps it's for the best. If she couldn't keep it up, after all..." Isabelle shrugged, and a group of gold bracelets jangled on her thin wrist.

Anna felt the heat of color in her cheeks, and she balled her hands. "She *could* keep it up. She was doing a great job."

"Obviously not great enough. My husband died, remember?" Isabelle put a hand on her hip and shifted her weight, her eyes narrowing.

"Mother," Ralph said in an uncertain voice. "Anna thinks perhaps it wasn't just negligence. Perhaps someone tampered with the equipment to make it break down. It's possible, isn't it?"

"Intentionally? That's absurd," Isabelle replied sharply. "Who would want to kill James? He was harmless." She paused, waved a jeweled hand, then added, "Mostly."

Ralph opened his mouth as if to say more but bit back his words with a cough. His face had grown even redder than Anna's usually did.

"I'm very sorry if my questions came across as rude." Anna took a step forward and tried to keep the anger out of her voice. "I've already spoken to the police about my ideas, and it looks like I'll be able to drop it now."

Two pairs of eyebrows went up in surprise.

"Well, that was sufficiently vague," Isabelle sniffed. "What does that mean?"

"Just that I will try to stay out of your way."

"Good. Well." Isabelle raised both hands in a mock shrug, shaking her head at Ralph. "That's all, then. I have a salon appointment before my lunch date."

"Date?" Ralph almost choked on the word.

"Not that it's any business of yours, but yes, I have a date. I'm not too old, you know."

"No, no, of course not. But, Mother, perhaps it might look better if you took some time, you know, to grieve."

"Pshaw." She pushed his hand off her arm and strode out of the room in a flurry of cotton, the sound of bangles, and the scent of Chanel No. 5.

Once again, Ralph looked like he was biting back what he wanted to say. After chewing on air for a second, he conceded. "Of course, whatever works for you." He gave Anna a helpless shrug. "We all grieve in our own way."

❧ 21 ☙

Anna took a deep breath and relaxed as soon as she entered the tiny sanctuary that the small square of yard behind Felicia's house had been transformed into. She was glad Felicia had called to invite her and Eoin over again. She couldn't help but compare the yard to the garden at Corey Bowman's house. Both gardens reflected the love and care that had gone into them. On the other hand, whoever tended Felicia's garden had a lot more skill.

"Kathy's the one with the green thumb, not me," Felicia said when Anna expressed her admiration. "But thank you. We do enjoy sitting out here."

"I can see why," Anna said appreciatively, keeping an eye on Eoin, who occupied himself by chasing the butterflies—fortunately without a net. Anna wasn't too worried about him catching one with his bare hands. "Now spill. Why did you call me over?"

Felicia raised an eyebrow and grinned. "I have more intel on Dean Harrison."

"Intel." Kathy snorted a laugh. "Is that what we're calling it these days?"

Felicia laughed too. "Okay, fine, gossip. But it could still be useful, couldn't it? Anna?"

"Oh, right, sorry." Anna pulled her attention back to the ladies at the table, realizing she'd been focusing a little too much on watching Eoin.

Felicia leaned over the table and put a hand on Anna's. "Forget the gossip. Anna, what's wrong? I can see it in your face. Something's bothering you."

Anna tried to smile, but it felt more like a grimace. She took a sip of her lemonade to cover it up. "I'm just worried about Eoin's future," she finally explained. "A lot is going on right now, a lot of unknowns."

"Well, that's the understatement of the year, dear. If we knew what the future held, we'd all be living life a little differently, wouldn't we?" Kathy replied.

"What's bothering you, specifically, Anna?" Felicia asked.

"My mom is in town."

"Ah."

"No, no, it's not like that. She just gave me some bad news."

"About?"

Anna let her eyes slide toward Eoin. Fortunately, the boy had jumped up to chase another butterfly.

"Ah." Felicia nodded. "I see. News on that front?"

Anna nodded and leaned in to whisper to them across the table. "His parents are making plans for him for the school year."

"Not good?"

Anna shook her head but closed her lips tight as Eoin turned and trotted back over. She gave him a big hug, which he promptly wriggled out of.

"I see." Kathy stood. "New plan, I'll be right back."

Anna looked questioningly at Felicia, who simply

shrugged.

In a few minutes, Kathy returned carrying a tray with wine glasses, white wine, and a purple liquor. "Forget the lemonade." Kathy placed the tray on a nearby bench. "You need to relax, take time to think about things. Have a Kir instead." As she spoke, she poured a bit of the purple liquor into a glass then topped it up with the white wine. She handed the glass to Anna then poured two more for herself and Felicia.

"A Kir?" Anna asked. "Angela mentioned drinking these. What are they?"

"A perfect afternoon drink, that's what." Kathy answered, raising her glass in a toast. "Cheers."

"It's crème de cassis, black currant liquor." Felicia took a sip. "It adds a sweet and tart taste to the wine. Go on, try it."

Anna took a sip then nodded her appreciation. "Sammy's going to be disappointed she wasn't here for this. It's quite a coincidence."

Kathy raised an eyebrow. "Why's that?"

"Angela had mentioned Kirs because that was what they drank when... on that tragic day." Anna shrugged. "Drinking this now is kind of like revisiting her story—like a tasty way to jog my memory about what she told me."

"Which reminds me." Felicia held up a finger. "The reason I invited you over—other than the pleasure of spending time with you both, of course. It's Dean."

"Again," Kathy said in a flat voice.

Felicia gave her a look. "Yes, again. Another friend saw him in town that morning."

"Not the winery?"

"No..." Felicia's voice wavered. "I suppose gossip isn't always the most accurate way to get information. This may have been later, of course, after he was at the winery."

"He certainly made the rounds. Busy boy that morning." Kathy laughed.

"He was having coffee with Anthony Middleton. He's one of the biggest business owners on the small business association."

"That sounds normal. Why wouldn't he be having coffee with a colleague?"

"Apparently, they looked suspicious."

Anna took another sip of her Kir to cover up her laugh. She looked over at Kathy, who simply shook her head with a smile.

Felicia huffed out a breath. "Look, he took the winery over from his father, who sank everything into it. It's all he has. He doesn't do much experimenting. Most of his sales are from traditional New Jersey wines."

"So?" Kathy raised her eyebrows in expectation.

"Angela *is* trying different grapes and blends," Anna said. "I guess that's a different approach for New Jersey wines."

"Exactly!" Felicia put her empty glass on the table with a bang then flinched at the sound. "Sorry, got a little too excited there. Anyway, Dean has some old vines, and I've been told that those are quite valuable."

"Valuable enough to kill over?" Anna asked skeptically, debating whether or not to share what she'd learned about Isabelle with her friends. "There are other suspects." She paused and chewed on her lip.

"Go on," Kathy prompted her.

"Well, his widow, obviously."

"Obviously." Felicia gave an exaggerated nod. "The widow is always the prime suspect. But that doesn't mean you can't consider other ideas, does it? Come on. Let's go talk to him." Felicia stood with a giggle.

Anna couldn't help but admire Felicia's enthusiasm, though she wasn't so sure about her logic. She kept her mouth shut about everything else she knew concerning Isabelle. The police would handle her. And in the meantime, Anna saw no harm in visiting another winery.

Dean Harrison's vines stretched down to the street, a brightly colored sign inviting guests in and directing them to the gravel parking lot. A large, colonial-style house stood back within the vines, a collection of barns lurking behind it. A few workers were already spread out among the vines, though Anna knew from Angela that the crush—the main harvesting season—wouldn't start for a few more weeks.

Felicia's car crunched over the gravel as she pulled into an empty spot. The winery was popular with locals and tourists alike, and none of the tables scattered around the wide porch were empty. Groups chatted and sipped as they enjoyed wine, cheese, and other snacks. A balcony on the second level also looked full, as Anna glimpsed more tables and customers through the upstairs windows. Inside, the barnlike structure housed a tasting bar and a small shop, much like Angela's.

A line of people had gathered at the tasting bar, but one person caught Anna's attention immediately. Ralph

Longhurst stood at one end, talking to a man whose rugged good looks could give Daniel Craig a run for his money.

Anna caught Ralph's eye and waved. Ralph blinked in surprise but managed a limp wave in return.

Felicia walked right up to the men. "Dean, I'm glad you're here. I want you to meet someone."

"Oh, you're Dean Harrison?" Anna stumbled over her words, caught off guard by Ralph's presence. "Hi, I'm Anna McGregor. I run Climbing Rose Cottage."

"Right, of course. I knew your aunt Louise. It's great to meet you."

"I was hoping we'd be able to chat," Felicia added, "privately."

Dean frowned in surprise but glanced around the room. "My wine steward has things covered out here. Do you want to step into the back room?"

The room he took them to seemed small and dark, though Anna soon realized it was bigger than it looked. The line of wine barrels along the walls made it feel smaller and added the heady scent of oak and must. Anna couldn't tell whether the barrels were decorative or stored wine, but she noticed that some had large, flat spoons hooked to them with metal chains.

A heavy wooden desk covered in papers and files and a few more wine tasting spoons sat at an angle across one corner of the room. Dean directed them all to find seats from the odd collection of chairs and stools that dotted the room then slid behind the desk. He pulled a bottle of wine out of somewhere and offered them a drink.

Eoin eagerly nodded. Anna laughed. "You wouldn't like it, Eoin. Trust me on that." She took a sip and changed her mind. It was sweet enough for the eight-year-old to enjoy.

"Alcoholic juice," Felicia whispered.

Dean nodded approvingly. "That's my main seller. It's

sweet, I know, not what you typically expect from a wine. But it's perfect for people who are new to wine, who are trying things out. Some of my customers eventually move on to more typical wines," he said bitterly, "but some just enjoy the pleasure of a sweet drink. There's nothing wrong with that. We have wines from blueberries, peaches..."

"Any made from grapes?" Felicia asked with a suspiciously sweet smile.

Dean nodded uncertainly. "Obviously."

"So you two are friends?" Anna nodded to Ralph and Dean.

"Sure," Ralph responded with enthusiasm before Dean had a chance to answer. "You know I run a distribution business. What with Dad in the 'business' as well, I've known Dean for most of my life." Ralph rolled his eyes and made air quotes around the word "business" to make sure there was no doubt in anyone's mind what he thought about his father's enterprise. "You know, Dad relied on Dean from the beginning, for advice, guidance, knowledge." He nodded and smiled at Dean.

Dean's reply carried more than a note of sourness. "James was one of those who graduated to better wines."

"We always loved your wines, Dean, the whole family."

"I'd love to hear more about your vineyard," Anna said sweetly. "Tell me, what kind of grapes do you grow?"

Dean beamed at the question. "My father started this winery thirty years ago. And he took it over from someone before him. We've always worked traditional New Jersey grapes here, and I plan to keep that up. I know some other winemakers in the area"—he shook his head, and his voice took on a darker tone—"are experimenting with different grapes, grapes from France, but I don't think there's anything wrong with what we've been doing right here for almost fifty years. Why mess with a good thing?"

"Why is that a problem for you?" Felicia asked.

"A problem? Of course it's not a problem."

"Then again," Felicia pointed out as if just thinking of the idea, "if people start expecting something different from New Jersey wines, they might not be as interested in yours. I see you're a very popular destination right now."

"And I doubt you could afford to replace all those vines, even if you wanted to," Anna added.

"If nothing else, you'd be out of business for years while you waited for the vines to mature," Felicia said.

Dean leaned forward in his seat, his hands resting heavily on the desk in front of him. His face turned from pink to rose to burgundy in a matter of seconds, but he said nothing.

Fearing for his health, Anna jumped in again. "I'm getting the sense that wine tends to be a family business throughout Cape May."

"Absolutely." Dean took a breath before continuing. "I've worked this place since I was a kid, when my dad owned it. Someday, I'll leave it to my son."

"Speaking of sons." Ralph nodded toward Eoin. "It's a pleasure to meet yours."

"Oh, no." Anna laughed. "Eoin is my cousin. He's visiting from Ireland."

"Ireland! How exciting. How are you enjoying your visit?"

"Oh, I love it here." Eoin jumped off his chair in his enthusiasm. "I love the beach and the ocean and the people and the library and the birds and the history and the—"

"He loves it here." Anna cut him off, figuring his list would go on for hours if she let him. "He loves everything about Cape May."

"Charming," Ralph replied. "How long will you be staying?"

Eoin looked down. "Not sure. Just till the end of the summer, I think. I s'pose they must have rebuilt my school by now."

"You don't want to go?"

Eoin shook his head.

"But you must have friends and family you miss."

Eoin looked more hopeful. "I miss my ma and pa and my friend Billy, oh, and my teachers!"

Anna felt a lump form in her throat as Eoin talked. He wasn't going to get back to see his teachers or his friends at school. *Why is Ralph asking all these questions anyway?*

"I do have a few questions I want to ask you both about Angela," Anna interrupted before Ralph could ask Eoin another question.

"Terrible." Ralph shook his head.

"Tragic," Dean agreed. "How could she let her equipment get so run-down? She always seemed so competent to me. I may not have liked her competition or her approach, but I always respected her as a professional."

"Anna doesn't think that's what happened." Ralph grinned.

"What? What else could it be?" Dean asked.

"Maybe someone tampered with the equipment," Ralph explained.

"That's a horrible idea. How could you even consider that, Anna? Think of how many people could have died."

Anna jumped in, tired of Ralph telling Dean what she was thinking. "I agree. It is terrible, but murder always is. And if it all happened that morning, the killer could've been pretty sure only one person would get hurt."

"What do you mean? If what happened that morning?"

"A line in the air circulation system was cut." Felicia leaned forward to place her mostly full cup of wine on the desk. "And James's oxygen monitor didn't work."

"But anyone could have picked up that monitor," Dean said.

Anna nodded. "That's true. James might not have been the intended victim."

Ralph smiled broadly. "Well, if you're here to check Dean's alibi, consider your job done. I was here with Dean all day Monday."

Dean frowned and opened his mouth but said nothing.

"Don't worry." Ralph waved a hand casually as he took another sip of wine, making a face. "It's okay. It doesn't matter. We weren't breaking the law or anything. Now, Eoin, tell me—"

"Thanks so much for your hospitality." Anna downed the last of her wine and tried to hide her grimace. "We really must be getting back. It was great meeting you."

❧ 23 ❧

"Thank you so much, Felicia. That gave me a lot to think about." Anna closed the passenger door of Felicia's car.

"My pleasure, dear. It's fun to watch you at work."

"Hardly," Anna scoffed. "Just poking around in the dark, more like."

Eoin waved as Felicia pulled away from Climbing Rose Cottage, moving his hands so hard his whole body shook.

"Come on, you. I need to get tea going for our guests. Want to help?"

"Can I?"

Anna laughed. It was nice to have an enthusiastic assistant, even if his assistance sometimes added to her workload rather than decreasing it.

"Anna!"

She paused on the top step to see Evan jogging up the front path.

"Hi! What are you doing here? Is something wrong?"

Evan stopped in his tracks. "Wrong? No. I... I just wanted to drop by, say hi. I was hoping we could talk."

"Absolutely, of course, right." Anna blinked as she shook her head. "Sorry. Pull up a chair." She perched at one of the tables on the porch used by her guests for breakfast and tea.

Eoin hugged Evan before running inside.

Evan laughed. "Where is he off to?"

"I hate to think." Anna smiled. "I did just invite him to help me get tea ready for the guests, so he's probably inside breaking my tea things."

Evan paused halfway through the process of sitting. "Is now a bad time?"

"It's fine." Anna waved a hand. "Sit. I don't have much time, though. I'm supposed to be serving tea in about ten minutes. But I baked everything this morning, so it's just a matter of setting the tables and boiling the water. Actually, I'm glad you're here."

"You are?" Evan's smile broadened. "Good."

"I still have questions about this murder."

"Ah. The murder. Right."

Anna frowned at Evan's attitude but forged ahead. "Have you found out anything about Isabelle taking that class?"

"Right, that. Thanks for the lead. We're interviewing her today."

"Has she admitted to being the killer yet?" Anna asked with a grin.

Evan returned her grin. "Nothing that easy, no. But you were right. She does have a little knowledge of mechanics. Nothing big, she just took one introductory course. But it might have been enough to teach her how to cut the line of the air ventilator and tamper with the oxygen meter."

"Plus she's been around wine and vineyards for so long she must know how dangerous it can be, how important it is to watch for low oxygen levels."

"Exactly. And she has a clear motive—and no alibi."

"Was she at the vineyard with James when it happened?"

Evan shook his head. "She says she was out shopping. But she has no receipts to back that up—says she didn't actually buy anything. We asked her what shops to see if any security footage put her in a store that morning, but she was vague, couldn't remember where she'd been. 'Just around,' she said."

"Well, that's suspicious on its own." Anna frowned. "I have noticed that she's been doing a lot of shopping recently, and dating. Oh!"

"What?"

"What if she started dating before James died? What if...?" Anna paused.

Evan finished her thought. "What if she wasn't shopping at all that morning but was with another man?" He shrugged. "It's possible. But why not tell us? We already think she has a motive. That would make it stronger, sure, but would also give her an alibi."

"Tell me this—how are you so sure the mechanics were tampered with that morning?"

"They must have been. Angela uses that room every day. It would take less than twenty-four hours for the carbon dioxide to build up. She would have noticed right away."

"What if none of the oxygen meters worked? Would she still notice?"

"First of all, yes, she would. She'd feel light-headed. She's been in the business long enough to know what that means."

"And second?"

"Second, they weren't all tampered with. Just the one that James used."

"Well, that's odd. What are the chances he'd pick up the broken one?"

Evan raised an eyebrow. "Exactly. How did the killer make that happen?"

Anna's phone buzzed, saving her from coming up with an answer. "Luke, hi."

Evan shifted on the seat next to her, turning away as if to give her some privacy.

"Hey. Just calling to see if you want to get dinner tonight." Luke's voice sounded strong, firm, confident.

"I'd love to, but my mom's still in town. I kind of want to spend time with her. Any chance you want to join us here?"

"Oh... um..." The confidence in Luke's voice dropped dramatically. "You know what, you spend time with your mom. We'll have plenty of time together. Don't worry."

Evan chuckled softly next to her as Anna hung up the phone.

"What?" she asked.

"Nothing, nothing. I was just thinking that our killer had to be someone who knew how to cut the ventilation line and was familiar with the oxygen meters—to recalibrate it quickly, on the spot. It's not hard to do if you know what you're doing, so we're looking at someone who works with this stuff—"

"Or took a class to learn about this stuff," Anna interrupted.

"True." Evan nodded. "That could be Dean or any other winemaker in the area. It's a long list of suspects, not just Isabelle."

"Hmm." Anna thought about that. "So the killer was definitely there that morning. There's still Rick Enright. If Isabelle was with another man that morning—"

Evan cut her off. "That's a big leap. We don't know that she was. She's still our prime suspect."

"Right. Of course. But just looking at other options, what about the man who taught Isabelle everything she knows about mechanics? The man who was furious at Angela and wanted her winery to go out of business?"

"The ex-boyfriend." Evan settled back into his chair. "It's not a strong motive."

"But does he have an alibi?"

Evan shrugged. "I don't know. I don't think we've interviewed him."

Anna tapped a finger against her chin. "That's an avenue I'd like to explore more."

"Anna." Evan toyed with his sunglasses. "I heard—"

"Anna, dear, you have guests congregating in the lounge," Mrs. McGregor cut Evan off.

Anna jumped up. "I'm so sorry, Evan. I do need to serve tea. What were you going to say?"

Barbara McGregor stepped out of the house. "Anna. Oh, hello."

"Ma'am." Evan nodded and backed away. "It's nothing, Anna. We'll talk another time. Ma'am," he repeated before turning and jogging back down to the street.

Mom raised an eyebrow. "Who was that handsome man?"

"Just a friend, Mom. Don't get all worked up. Come on. Let's find out what kind of trouble Eoin's getting into in the kitchen." As she walked into the house, Anna glanced back to see Evan walking briskly away. *What was he going to tell me?*

$\maltese$ 24 $\maltese$

"I think that's all of it." Barbara put away the last clean teacup.

"Perfect. Thank you so much for your help, Mom. It's amazing how much faster cleaning up goes with two people." Anna glanced at Eoin, sitting at the kitchen table.

His mouth was already full of mac 'n' cheese, and he was trying to fit in another forkful.

"Especially when the second person isn't Eoin."

Her mom laughed. "You know he tries."

Eoin looked up, finally realizing they were talking about him. "Hmmmm?"

"Chew your food then swallow it then try to talk." Barbara shook her head. "He reminds me so much of you at that age."

"Me?" Anna asked, surprised. "I don't remember ever eating like that."

"No? Once you started field hockey, you always came home ravenous. It died down a bit as you got older, but when you were young, oh yes. And the reading!" Her mom burst into a fit of laughter as she made her way over to the table and sat next to Eoin. "Maybe you weren't quite as enthusiastic as Eoin, but you loved to read."

"That I do remember." Anna slid into the chair opposite her mother. "I still love to read, and the books Aunt Louise collected over her lifetime are amazing. There's enough in this house to keep both Eoin and me occupied for years!"

Eoin nodded, a drop of yellow cheese slowly running down his chin. He mumbled something that sounded like, "I mlove the mooks here."

"Chew your food then swallow," Barbara repeated.

Eoin swallowed loudly and grinned at her.

She laughed and leaned forward to ruffle Eoin's hair. "Eoin, we need to talk about something."

The innocence and happiness in his eyes as he looked at Anna's mother made Anna's spirits plunge. It was not good news he was about to hear, and she worried how he might react.

Anna spoke up. "Eoin, you know that your parents love you very much, right?"

Eoin nodded.

Anna continued. "And they love each other very much too. I know they do. But sometimes, with grown-ups, even when they love one another, they need to be apart from each other."

Eoin furrowed his brow. "Whatcha mean?"

Barbara jumped in. "Your parents are going to be spending some time apart."

"How much time?" Eoin asked in a soft voice.

Anna put her hand over his. "It could be a very long time. No one knows what the future holds, but for now, your father is moving out of your house."

Eoin swallowed loudly again. "I don't understand."

"I know. I'm not sure I do either. Adults are complicated, and they do strange things. But the most important thing for you to know is that they both really love you."

Eoin nodded uncertainly. "So where will I live?"

Anna glanced at her mother, who took over. "Tell me, what do you think of starting somewhere new? Maybe starting at a new school?"

Eoin's eyes widened. "But what about my friends?"

Barbara nodded. "You can still be friends with them. You can stay in touch with your friends. You can talk on the phone or email or chat. There are lots of ways to talk to your friends. And at a new school, you can make more friends."

"But what if I don't make any new friends?"

"You made friends here, didn't you?"

Eoin's eyes lit up. "BethAnne." His voice took on that dreamy quality it tended to whenever he talked about BethAnne.

Barbara faltered and gave Anna an enquiring look. Anna nodded, so Barbara continued, "Yes, like BethAnne. You're such a sweet, interesting young man. You'll make new friends without any trouble at all. I'm sure of it."

Eoin thought about that for a moment while stirring what was left of his mac 'n' cheese with his fork. He dug the fork in and pulled out a mouthful then paused, the food halfway to his mouth. "So where will I live?" he asked again.

Anna looked at her mom, who simply shrugged. "I'm not sure, Eoin. I understand your parents are looking at several good schools in Dublin."

"Dublin?" Eoin's eyebrows shot up. "But that's so far from home."

"It's a little far, yes. But that's okay because you can have a room there. You can stay at your school. Wouldn't that be fun?"

Eoin's fork shook then tipped over, the mac 'n' cheese flinging out over the table. He tried to nod, but it turned into more of a shudder as his eyes filled with tears. "So... I won't... be going home?"

"Oh, no, Eoin." Anna leaned over and wrapped an arm around him. "Of course you'll go home. It's just that when school starts, you'll have somewhere new and fun to go."

She felt Eoin nod again, then it turned into a shudder.

Eoin sniffed then sniffed again. He pulled away from her. "'Scuse me," he mumbled as he ran out of the room.

❦ 25 ❦

"That was hard. Thank you so much for coming over, Sammy." Anna dropped onto the sofa next to Sammy and slid down until her head rested against the back.

"Ugh. Poor kid. He's terrified, and I don't blame him."

"He feels abandoned."

Sammy raised an eyebrow. "For good reason. Not great parents, are they?"

"I don't want to judge them. I don't know what they're going through."

"Well, they're not putting Eoin first, and that's bad."

"I guess."

Barbara came into the lounge from the kitchen. "I'm going to bed myself, Anna. Everything's cleared up in the kitchen."

"Now? It's pretty early."

"After that experience, I'm exhausted. I plan to take a long soak in that fabulous tub of yours then settle into bed with a book."

"Do you want me to bring you up a cup of tea, Mrs. McGregor?" Sammy asked.

"That's not necessary, dear, but thank you!"

Barbara kissed the top of Anna's head and left the room.

Sammy leaned over and put an arm around Anna. "Are you going to be okay?"

"I feel so bad for him."

"I know, me too. Don't worry. We'll figure something out."

Anna leaned her head on Sammy's shoulder. "And how about you? Have you figured out who's been stealing from you?"

Anna felt Sammy's head shake no. "I've been watching everyone like a hawk, but I haven't caught anyone in the act. On the plus side, nothing else's gone missing. But I can't keep this up. I need to come up with a new plan."

The two friends sat in silence for a moment, each lost in their thoughts, thoughts that were rudely interrupted by the doorbell.

"Who could that be at this time of night?" Anna grumbled as she dragged herself off the sofa.

Sammy laughed. "It's only eight o'clock, Anna. How old are you?"

Anna rolled her eyes and ran to get the door.

Corey Bowman stood on the step. "Good evening, Anna. I hope you don't mind my stopping by. I brought a gift." He held up a bottle of white wine.

"Come in, come in. You remember my friend Sammy." Anna escorted Corey into the lounge and gestured to a chair.

"I was worried our last conversation did not end on the best of notes." Corey took a seat. He glanced at the wine he still held. "I hope we can enjoy this. It's a semidry white blend from a local winery."

"Local?" Anna chewed on her lips. "Oh, I have an idea." She ran to the kitchen but returned promptly with a bottle of crème de cassis and three wine glasses.

"Why do you have that?" Sammy sat forward on the sofa.

"One of my guests came down to attend a wedding. They were given it at the event but didn't want it, so they gave it to me."

"May I?" Corey took the bottle from Anna. As he worked the cork out of the wine bottle, he said, "I've heard through the grapevine that you like to ask questions about murders."

Anna shifted uncomfortably in her seat. "I guess you could say that, though I really don't like the way it sounds. Angela just asked for my help. She knew she wasn't negligent. As it turns out, she was right."

"She was?"

"Oh, I don't know if that's public information yet."

Sammy widened her eyes.

"Anyway, I just ask a few questions, learn about the people involved, consider the timeline, that sort of thing."

"And I'm sure the last story I told you about James bounced me to the top of your suspect list." Corey laughed. He handed out the glasses then held his up. "Cheers."

"Cheers." Anna smiled. "No, nothing like that."

"I thought of something else you might be interested in," Corey said.

Sammy leaned forward eagerly. "What?"

"It's about Dean Harrison. Do you know him?"

"I do. He's friendly with Ralph, I noticed."

"Hah." Corey coughed out a laugh. "Friendly? Hardly."

"What do you mean? Oh, that's good." Sammy opened

her eyes wide again as she tasted her drink. "Sorry, what do you mean?"

"Dean's winery is big business," Corey explained.

"I saw that he was pretty busy yesterday," Anna agreed. "But I can't imagine he distributes much outside of New Jersey."

"Well, maybe not yet, but he's trying to expand—selling more of his fruit wines, sweet wines."

"How much interest is there in those types of wine, outside New Jersey?" Sammy asked.

"He does a great job of marketing and bringing visitors to Cape May. That's important to the town and the region."

"I could see that. But what does that have to do with the Longhursts?" Anna asked.

"They're in the business—well, James was in the business—of bringing in foreign wines. Dean saw that as competition."

"Angela said it wasn't."

"Angela has a good head on her shoulders. It really isn't competition," Corey agreed.

"Then what's Dean upset about?" Sammy asked.

"He didn't look upset when talking with Ralph," Anna pointed out.

Corey shrugged and took another sip of his Kir. "He has plans, grand visions. He has this idea that his wines will pick up in popularity, prove the value of New Jersey wines."

"It's not so strange. Angela has a similar vision, I guess," Anna said.

"But very different kinds of wine," Corey pointed out.

Anna nodded and took another sip. "Why are you telling us this?"

"You said you asked questions about the people involved. That was something I thought you should know about James. He wasn't all love and joy. He did have some enemies."

"Dean Harrison, you mean?" Sammy asked.

"For one. Dean asked him to help distribute his wines, and James rebuffed him."

"He wasn't a distributor," Anna pointed out.

"True, but instead of encouraging Dean to work with Ralph, who was a distributor, he simply scoffed and said he didn't want to be connected with wines like Dean's."

"Ooh, that's harsh," Sammy said.

"Very," Corey agreed.

"But now Ralph is working with Dean?" Anna asked.

Corey shrugged. "I hadn't heard that, but perhaps he is. Ralph was always different from his father, more willing to work with people, to get along. To grow the business, you know."

"Makes sense." Anna nodded.

"James wouldn't distribute Dean's wine, and Angela was selling wines that directly competed with Dean's vision of the New Jersey wine market," Sammy said. "Now James is dead, Angela is going out of business, and Ralph is distributing Dean's wine."

Corey raised an eyebrow and took another sip.

ॐ   26   ॐ

nna waited on a bench outside the municipal offices. She didn't have much time—her mother was getting breakfast set out, Eoin was refusing to come out of his room, and she had agreed to meet Luke for coffee later that morning—but she had to talk to Evan.

A row of brightly colored dahlias lined the pavement in front of the building, adding cheer to an otherwise-simple space. Whoever was doing their gardening had a clear talent, though she missed the love that shone through gardens like Corey's or Kathy's. With her back to the building, Anna raised her face to the morning sun, closing her eyes and taking a deep breath in an attempt to be patient. Finally, she heard footsteps coming up the path along the side of the building that led to the police station. She opened her eyes to watch Evan cut across the grass toward her.

"Anna, I'm surprised to see you at this time of the morning," he greeted her as he leaned over to peck her on the cheek. He joined her on the bench. "You're usually swamped with breakfast."

"I know, right?" Anna laughed. "Maybe it's not such a bad thing having my mom around to help."

"I'm glad to see you." He put a hand out then pulled it back. "What do you need? Your message said it was important."

Her smile faded. "It is. I've been poking around into the murder a bit more."

"I thought you'd figured out that Isabelle did it." Evan looked quizzical. "I passed that tip on to Detective Walsh, and he's following up on it."

"I'm glad to hear it, and maybe that's it." Anna shrugged and looked out over the garden. "It's just, the more I learn, the more I realize that other people had means and motives too."

Evan let out a breath. "All right, I'll bite. Who?"

"Dean Harrison."

"Dean Harrison, who runs the winery just outside town?"

Anna nodded. "That's the man."

Evan shifted on the bench, folding his arms across his chest. "I see. And what would his motive be?"

Evan's attitude made it quite clear he only asked to placate her, not because he thought the suggestion had any merit, but she forged ahead anyway. "It turns out he and James had a conflict not too long ago. James rejected Dean's request to distribute his wines—"

"But James wasn't a distributor," Evan cut her off.

"True, but he didn't just say that, or suggest Dean work with Ralph, who was. He insulted Dean's wines, said he'd never work with wines like that."

Evan shrugged. "That's not a reason to kill someone."

"I know." Anna moved her head from side to side. "But then there's also Dean's competition with Angela. Angela is producing different kinds of wines, wines that could potentially, eventually put Dean out of business."

"Sounds like usual business competition to me. I understand Ralph was always a little competitive with his father. He would have picked Dean up as a client just because his father rejected Dean."

Anna laughed and looked down. "I know some parent-child relationships like that. Maybe you're right."

"Maybe." He lowered his head to look her in the eye and smiled warmly. "But I won't discount your ideas, Anna. I know better than that. We're still focusing on Isabelle, but I did find some interesting background on Rick Enright." Evan glanced around the empty yard before continuing. "It's not public knowledge. I probably shouldn't be sharing it with you."

"I don't want you to break any codes of secrecy or anything," Anna said, though she couldn't hide her curiosity.

"I won't give you the details, but basically Rick has a record."

Anna furrowed her brow. "Aren't arrest records public information?"

"He was never charged." Evan glanced around again. "It was a domestic dispute, and in the end, the woman involved chose not to press charges. He was never actually arrested, so there's no official record, which means I can't share anything with the public. It's just internal notes."

"A domestic dispute? What does that mean?"

Evan's jaw moved as he looked down at his hands. "It means violence of some sort, right? You don't need me to tell you that. And I definitely won't tell you the name of the woman involved."

"Violence? And a woman was involved?" Anna's eyes

opened wide. "You're saying he hit a woman he was involved with?"

Evan nodded once but said, "I'm not telling you anything. Like I said, this isn't public information. But I was interested, since you asked about him."

"And it turns out he has a history of violence against the women in his life. Interesting."

"It's a pretty big leap, though, from domestic violence to premeditated murder."

"True. But it's still interesting. Angela says he was really mad at her when they broke up. He could have stewed over his anger for a while then taken action."

"And in his effort to get back at Angela, James paid the ultimate price?" Evan shrugged. "It's plausible, I suppose."

Anna jumped up then leaned down to peck Evan on the cheek. "Thank you for this—and for taking me seriously. Now I need to get back."

"Breakfast to serve?" Evan smiled.

"That and an unhappy eight-year-old to cheer up."

❧ 27 ❧

After breakfast had been cleared away, Anna finally succeeded in convincing Eoin to come out of his room. He slid onto a chair at the kitchen table, his head hanging toward his hands.

"Hey there, buddy. Do you want a muffin?"

Eoin shrugged but didn't respond.

Anna put a muffin on a plate in front of him along with a glass of orange juice. Eoin toyed with the muffin, tearing a few pieces off, but didn't eat.

"Where's that famous appetite we're always teasing you about?"

He shrugged again.

"I'm just finishing up here. Do you want to go out somewhere together?"

He dipped his head. "Sure."

"Well, that was hardly an excited response. Come on, where do you want to go? To the beach?"

"Eh."

"To the docks?"

"Eh."

"To the library?"

Eoin's eyes lit up for a second, then his face dropped again. "Hmm, maybe later."

"You mean when BethAnne is back?" Anna nudged him. "Okay, how about if we just walk and talk?"

"Okay." Eoin slid off his stool, but Anna was relieved to see him shove half of the muffin into his mouth.

They walked east along Columbia Avenue then turned right then left then right again, wandering without paying attention to where they were going. Anna tried to drag Eoin out of his funk by pointing out fun features on some of the houses, birds perched in trees, even large bugs on the sidewalk—all things that only yesterday would have had him bouncing up and down with excitement. Today, the most she got from him was a nod, sometimes a grunt.

"Oh, Eoin. It will be okay, I promise."

He stopped and looked up at her. "D'you really promise?"

She paused, thinking about her response. She had no idea what his future held, and she had to admit, being packed off to a boarding school didn't sound like a whole lot of fun. She crouched down to look him in the eyes. "Look, I know it doesn't sound very good right now. But I do promise that it will get better. You will make friends at your new school. You'll still have both your parents, who love you very much, and you'll still have me."

"I will?" He looked up at her hopefully.

She laughed and pulled him into a tight hug. "Always, Eoin, always. Even when you're in Ireland, and I'm here in Cape May, we'll talk on the phone and write letters and emails. And I'll send you pictures." She pulled away to look him in the eye. "You'll write back to me, right? And send me pictures?"

He nodded, but tears started forming in his eyes again. "I don't want to leave," he whispered.

"I know, honey. I don't want you to leave either." She hugged him tightly. "Come on, let's see where we are."

Anna realized they were following a path similar to the one she took the other day to the Restful Retreat Inn. The thought of the inn brought Isabelle to mind. Evan had said Detective Walsh was pursuing her lead. *Does that mean they arrested her or brought her in for questioning? Or does it simply mean they're digging into her past more?*

Her mind was so focused on Isabelle that she almost didn't recognize the man walking briskly toward them.

Instead of stepping to the side to make room on the sidewalk, as she normally would have done, Anna stepped into the middle of the path to block his way. "Rick?"

Rick stopped, startled. "Yeah?" He glanced back and forth between Anna and Eoin, then his gaze landed on Anna, and his face cleared. "I know you. You were at Angela's winery the other day."

Anna nodded. "You were just leaving as I arrived, and Angela seemed pretty upset."

Rick scoffed. "Upset. The only thing she gets upset about is that winery of hers. Me leaving? Nah, that doesn't upset her." He glanced down at Eoin, who was focused on his feet.

"Whatcha looking at there, little man?"

Eoin looked up at him but without his usual smile. "Nothing."

Rick laughed. "That's what they always say when they're up to something, isn't it?"

"I was surprised you were even at the winery the other day." Anna kept her voice casual, just one neighbor asking after another. "I would have thought you'd be avoiding the place."

Rick seemed to accept her question as one of concern rather than prying. "Yeah, no kidding. I was only there to grab some stuff I'd left behind. That's it. You're right. It's not somewhere I want to hang out right now." He nodded and moved as if to continue walking.

Anna put a hand on his arm. "Was that the first time you'd been back since you and Angela split up?"

He stopped and lowered his brows, pulling his arm away from Anna. "The first time? What business is it of yours if I go back to talk to my girlfriend?"

"Your ex-girlfriend," Anna reminded him.

"Whatever." He looked Anna up and down, as if trying to figure her out. "Yeah, I've tried to talk to her a few times. She wouldn't listen. Maybe this tragedy is exactly what she needs to get her priorities right. You'd think that winery was the be-all and end-all, the way she puts all her time into it. At least now she'll have time to focus on other things."

"That's what she thought you'd say."

"Why are you asking these questions?" He stepped toward her, and Anna saw his right arm raise slightly, his hand tightening into a fist.

Her reaction was instinctual and immediate. She stepped in front of Eoin to block him from Rick and flinched at the same time.

Rick's eyes opened wide, and he stepped back, his hand falling loose by his side.

As soon as he stepped back, Anna realized how foolish she looked. And what a terrible mistake she'd just made.

"Are you afraid of me?" Rick asked, taking one more step back. "Why'd you even stop me? And why are you afraid of me? What did Angela say?"

Anna felt the heat rising in her face, embarrassed by her reaction. "Nothing, Angela didn't say anything."

Rick looked away, letting out a breath. "No?" He looked back at Anna, and his eyes narrowed. "You've been palling around with that cop. That's it. I know you have. Everyone's seen you. Did he tell you something?"

Anna held her breath as she shook her head, unable to say the lie out loud.

Rick made a face and nodded. "I knew it. You can't trust the cops. Well, I'll see about that."

28

Eoin took Anna's hand and looked up at her, his expression full of concern. "Are you okay, Cousin Anna? That man was very angry."

Anna pulled Eoin into a hug. "I'm fine, honey, thank you. And yes, yes he was. Come on, let's keep walking."

Anna could still feel the adrenaline pumping through her veins but refused to let her fear prevent her from focusing on Eoin. She held his hand tightly as they walked, continuing to point out particular flowers or birds that once would have had him jumping up and down with excitement.

After a couple of blocks, Eoin pointed. "Look, a butterfly!"

"Yes!" Anna squeezed his hand. "Isn't it beautiful?"

Eoin nodded but held onto her hand. A few more yards down the street, Eoin pointed again. "What type of flower is that, Cousin Anna?"

Anna crouched next to him to look closely then pulled out her phone. "Let's see. I believe... yes, it's a tiger lily. Very dramatic, isn't it?"

Eoin nodded, slipped his hand out of hers, and pulled his notebook out of his pocket. Anna's shoulders relaxed, and a smile crept across her face. If he was taking notes, he must be feeling better.

They continued their walk, identifying birds and flowers along the way. Some Eoin recognized. Others Anna would look up on her phone and Eoin would write down in his notebook. As they walked, the neighborhood gradually changed. They'd entered a residential part of the town, where impressive houses stood in vast plots of lush green lawn. A few houses still adhered to the traditional Victorian style, but Anna and Eoin also passed brick colonials, cottages with cedar siding, even one in an art deco style. After the next right turn, the ocean opened up in front of them. Anna took a deep breath and noticed Eoin doing the same.

"Just seeing the ocean relaxes me," Anna explained.

Eoin nodded. "Me too."

She took his hand and held it tightly as they walked the last block toward the beach. When they reached Beach Avenue, she realized they'd come out right next to the Restful Retreat Inn. They were waiting to cross the road when a disturbance behind them caught her attention.

"Do be careful with that," Isabelle was complaining to Ralph. "They were gifts."

"I am, Mother," Ralph answered through gritted teeth, carrying a box awkwardly.

Isabelle breezily floated down to the sidewalk without a care in the world—until she saw Anna. "You! Are you stalking us? Was it your fault I spent most of yesterday in a police station with my lawyer?"

Anna's eyebrows went up. "Hello. I'm not stalking you. I'm going for a walk with my cousin."

Eoin peeped out from behind Anna and waved.

"How cute," Isabelle said dryly. "Come on, Ralph. Hurry up."

A staffer from the inn came out carrying a small suitcase and loaded it into the trunk of a large black BMW sedan parked in front of the inn. Isabelle barely acknowledged the staff member but simply waited next to the back door. The staffer trotted over and opened the door for her. She climbed in, and he slammed the door shut. Anna caught a glimpse of a suited chauffeur sitting behind the wheel.

"I'm sorry about my mother," Ralph said quietly to Anna. "It's like she's a different person since my father died."

"We all suffer in different ways, I suppose."

"I suppose." Ralph lowered his eyebrows. "Though I admit, she doesn't seem to be particularly suffering."

"Do you know what happened during the police interviews? Do they still consider her a suspect?"

Ralph shrugged. "Who knows what the police are thinking? All I know is that once her lawyer joined the conversation, she got out of there lickety-split. I bet they didn't have enough to charge her."

"I'm sorry. I know she's your mother, but some clues point at her being involved."

"That's absurd." Ralph scoffed. "Mother doesn't have it in her." He looked sideways at Anna. "This *was* your doing, wasn't it?" He grinned. "Has it occurred to you that you might be barking up the wrong tree?"

Anna recoiled at the comment. "I'm not a dog chasing a squirrel, Ralph. Yes, it's true. When I find information that might be useful, I share it with the police. It's up to them to figure out what it all means."

Ralph's smile spread. "Helping the police, huh? Is that what you call it?" He laughed. "Look, I might as well tell you. I wasn't with Dean the morning my father died. I lied to give him an alibi—you were sniffing around, and things didn't look good for him. He's a good friend, you know."

"Why are you telling me this now?"

Ralph shrugged, but there was a glint in his eye. "Perhaps I just want to send you off chasing another squirrel instead of my mother." He looked around then back at her. "Dean asked me to lie, to say I was with him. I don't know why."

A knock on the car window, from the inside, drew their attention back to the vehicle.

"Gotta run." Ralph wiggled his eyebrows. "Good luck with your investigation." He jogged to the other side of the car and slid into the back seat next to his mother.

Anna watched as the car glided smoothly away. She looked down at Eoin, who returned her gaze with wide eyes.

"It seems like everyone has something to hide, doesn't it? But who was willing to kill to protect their secret?"

29

Eoin's feet dragged as he pulled himself up the porch steps, and Anna couldn't blame him. They'd been walking for over an hour. She was exhausted too. But she would rather see Eoin exhausted than sad.

"All right, Eoin, jump onto a chair, and I'll go inside and grab your book and an iced tea."

She watched as Eoin crawled up onto an Adirondack chair then popped into the house. Eoin's latest book still lay on the coffee table in the lounge, where he'd left it. She poured a glass of tea from the urn she kept in the dining room for guests then took that and the book back out to Eoin.

"You hungry?" she asked as he slid back into the chair, book on his lap, iced tea in his hands.

He nodded.

"I bet. You didn't eat much this morning. All right, I'll go make you some lunch. Mac 'n' cheese?"

Eoin's eyes finally lit up at the mention of his favorite lunch, and he nodded again, a hint of a smile on his face.

Anna kissed the top of his curly red head and went back inside, following the sounds of what she hoped was her mother in the kitchen.

Barbara looked up as Anna came through the swinging door. "How's Eoin?" she asked.

The question was exactly what Anna would have expected, but the tone wasn't. Her mother's eyes twinkled, and she couldn't hide the grin that crept onto her face.

"Fine," Anna answered warily. "Just what you'd expect. Why? What do you have up your sleeve?"

Barbara laughed. "I've been busy this morning. After seeing Eoin's reaction—and yours, dear." Barbara put a hand on Anna's arm. "I hadn't realized how close you two had become."

Anna shrugged. "I know it's only been a few months, but I really love that boy. And I hate to see him so depressed, so spill."

"Well, I convinced your father to call his cousin."

"That couldn't have been easy." Anna pulled a box of mac 'n' cheese from the cupboard.

"No, but I was very persuasive." Barbara grinned again. "Anyway, they chatted about the options for Eoin's future, and it's not definite... there would still be a lot to work out... but both of his parents agree, so that's the big thing—"

"Mom! Out with it! What are you saying?"

"What would you think of Eoin staying here, in Cape May? Would you be willing to serve as his guardian for a longer time?"

Anna dropped the box of mac 'n' cheese she'd just opened onto the table, dry macaroni spilling out every-where. "Would I? Are you kidding?" She cut across the room and threw her arms around her mother. "How did you do it? I can't believe you did all this just this morning!"

Barbara laughed as she returned her daughter's hug. "It's not done, trust me. But his parents agree, and that's the first step. And really, Anna." She pulled away to look Anna in the eye. "I'm sorry I didn't think of it sooner. I truly hadn't realized how close you and Eoin have become, how much he loves being here."

"And how much I love having him here. I know, it's kind of surprising. You'd think I'd want more freedom."

Barbara nodded. "Raising a boy his age is a lot of work, dear. Are you sure you're up for it?"

Anna laughed. "Am I sure I'm up for it? No, definitely not sure. But am I sure I want to try? Absolutely."

"Okay, well, we have a few more calls to make." Her mother pulled out her phone and started tapping notes. "We need to think about Eoin's visa, for one thing, your legal status as his guardian. That will require a lawyer, for sure."

Anna waited a few minutes while her mother tapped out her list of everything they needed to do but finally couldn't wait anymore.

In a soft voice, she asked, "Do you think I should Eoin?"

Barbara looked up, and Anna could tell she was about to say no. "It might be premature. We don't want to get him too excited. What if we can't get his visa sorted out, for example? What if—" She stopped, seeing something in Anna's eyes. "Yes," she relented. "Go tell Eoin."

Anna didn't wait for her mother to reconsider. She ran out to the porch. Eoin still sat in the large chair, his book closed on his lap.

"Eoin, you're not reading. Why not?"

Eoin shook his head and shrugged.

Anna knelt next to his chair and put a hand on his arm.

"Tell me, do you like it here? In Cape May, I mean, with me?"

Eoin nodded, and his eyes filled with tears.

Anna quickly continued. "Would you like to stay here? You could go to school here instead of back in Ireland."

Eoin furrowed his brow. "Whatcha mean?"

"Well." Anna tried to choose her words carefully. "You know how I told you how much your parents love you, even though they're moving apart from each other?"

Eoin nodded again.

"They love you so much that when they heard you didn't want to go to a boarding school in Dublin, they talked with my parents about what other options you had, and one option is staying right here."

Eoin's eyes widened, and his hand holding his iced tea began to shake. Anna took the glass and put it on a nearby table.

"Could I really stay here?" he asked softly.

Anna nodded. "If you want to. And only for as long as you want. You could stay for the next school year and see if you like it."

Eoin's expression changed slowly, but the transformation was complete. His eyes brightened. His tears dried. A grin split across his face, and red blotches appeared on his cheeks. He shook his head and opened his mouth, but nothing came out.

Anna laughed. "Eoin, I do believe this is the first time I've seen you at a loss for words."

Eoin slid forward in his chair and wrapped his arms around Anna.

She hugged him back tightly. "Come on. Let's tell my mom you agree."

"Woohoo!" Eoin sang out as he jumped down from the chair then kept jumping as he made his way across the porch. "I'm staying... I'm staying," he sang out as he jumped.

Anna couldn't help but laugh out loud. The boy's joy was truly infectious.

"Anna." Her mother's voice cut across their laughter. Barbara leaned out the front door, the phone in her hand. "There's a call for you. It's the police."

Expecting Evan's voice on the other end of the line, Anna grabbed the phone. "Hey, want to hear some great news?"

"Ms. McGregor?" an unfamiliar male voice responded.

"Oh, yes. This is Anna McGregor."

"This is Patrolman John Cornish. I'm calling because we received a complaint about you."

"A complaint?" Anna asked.

Both her mother and Eoin stepped forward when she said that.

"Yes, ma'am. We've started a report and will be looking into it further to see if there are grounds to file a formal report. I need you to come down to the station as soon as possible."

30

Anna walked slowly up the path alongside the municipal building that led to the police station. Her feet dragged, and her heart fluttered nervously. Even the dahlias, which looked so cheerful earlier that morning, seemed to sag. She hesitated before going in. *Who would have filed a report against me?* Unfortunately, several people came to mind. She'd been poking her nose into other people's business quite a lot recently—most recently, Isabelle. She had been pretty angry and had blamed Anna for her afternoon in the station.

Anna pushed the glass door open and stepped cautiously inside. The entrance was bright but small. White-painted cement-block walls rose from a floor covered in industrial gray carpeting. A low wall created a sort of welcome desk for visitors, though the plexiglass that protected whoever stood behind it made it slightly less welcoming.

A uniformed patrolman came through a doorway behind the low wall. "Ms. McGregor?"

Anna nodded. "I came as soon as you called. I'm not really sure what's going on."

The man nodded. "I'm Patrolman John Cornish. Thank you for coming in. Please follow me."

Anna followed him along a corridor with the same whitewashed walls to a utilitarian room cluttered with desks and filing cabinets. Clearly a room designed for work, not for entertaining members of the public, it felt cold, austere. John gestured to a chair next to one of the desks, but Anna had stopped paying attention.

Her entire focus was on Evan. He sat at one of the desks, his fingers hovering over a keyboard but not typing, his brow furrowed. He'd glanced over when Anna had entered the room then had looked away immediately. He stood, gathered a few papers from his desk, and moved toward her. She smiled, expecting the familiar greeting. Instead, he passed right by her without saying a word—without even making eye contact.

What is going on? Did I commit a crime? Anna's breath caught, and she looked at Cornish.

He simply gestured again to the chair. That time she sat. He took the chair behind the desk, reached over, and grabbed a brown paper file folder. He opened it onto his desk, picking up a sheet of paper and looking over it.

Finally, after what seemed like ages, he spoke. "Tell me, what do you know about Rick Enright?"

"Rick?" Anna tried to focus on Patrolman Cornish and his question. "Rick?" she repeated, confused.

John Cornish nodded.

"Oh, um... not much, really. I'm friends with Angela Nelson, his former girlfriend." Anna paused, expecting another question or an explanation, but Cornish sat silently, simply watching her. "Right," she continued. "And, uh, I know he's a mechanic. I guess that's about it." She shrugged and shook her head.

"Have you ever spoken to him?" Cornish jotted down a quick note.

"No. Oh, I mean yes. Briefly. We just passed on the street and exchanged a few words, that's all."

"Did he threaten you at that time?"

Anna's mind flew back to an image of Rick's balled fist, of her jumping in front of Eoin. "No..." She dragged the word out. "I wouldn't say threaten. He scared me a little. Wait, why? I don't understand. I thought someone was complaining about me."

"Yes, ma'am, that's correct. Can you tell me why you felt threatened by him?"

"I don't know, the way he moved. He balled his hand into a fist."

"Like this?" Cornish balled his hand into a fist and held it by his side.

"Yes." Anna let out a light laugh and shook her head. "But when he did it, it scared me."

"Why was that?"

"Well, he stepped toward me. You can imagine. A big guy forming a fist and stepping toward me. Of course I was scared."

Cornish wrote a few more notes. "So there was no other reason you had for suspecting he might have a temper?"

Anna's thoughts spun in furious circles. There was another reason, a reason she wasn't supposed to know. She tried to keep her poker face on. She kept her mouth shut and shook her head.

"Uh-huh." Cornish nodded and jotted down a note.

"What's going on, Patrolman Cornish? Can you please tell me?" Anna leaned toward him.

He leaned back and tapped the papers into a neat pile

then stuck them into the folder. "Mr. Enright believes you had access to confidential police records and that the leak of those records has negatively impacted his standing within the community—records that, by the way, document a charge that was dropped." He looked around the empty room. "Ms. McGregor, I investigated that charge when it was first made. There was nothing to it. Mr. Enright never hit anyone. That was why the charges were dropped— because they were made up."

"Oh."

"It happens. A jilted lover wants revenge. She claims he hit her."

"That's a terrible thing to do."

"It is. It should never have gone as far as it did. But these things happen. Fortunately, I was able to ferret out the truth. Her story didn't add up. She kept changing the timelines then changed what she was accusing him of. She finally admitted it wasn't true."

"I see."

He looked at her, blinked, nodded once. "Yes, you do, don't you?"

Anna realized she'd been tricked into admitting she knew about the charge. Her hand flew to her mouth, but it was too late. "What happens now?"

"The officer—or patrolman—who gave you this information will be disciplined. I don't suppose you care to tell me who that was?"

Anna shook her head.

"No, I didn't think so. I also don't think I need you to tell me."

"Am I being charged with anything?"

"No, you're not, at least not by me. But I can't speak for Rick. If he thinks you're spreading unsubstantiated rumors around town about him based on this false charge, he has the right to sue you."

Anna swallowed back her retort. This was not something to take lightly.

"Come on, I'll show you out."

Anna followed Patrolman Cornish silently as he led the way back to the front door. He pushed the door open for her and held it as he glanced at the sky. "Take care in the storm. I heard it's going to be a big one."

What once had been a beautiful day had turned gray and cloudy. A chilling wind buffeted the tops of the trees, promising worse to come. She waved one hand in a weak gesture of thanks and headed back home, her head down. She faced the risk of a lawsuit, but more importantly, Evan was in trouble, and it was all her fault.

❧ 31 ❧

The curtain at the front window twitched as she walked up the path to Climbing Rose Cottage. Barbara jumped on her as soon as she came in, dragging her into the lounge.

"What happened? Are you okay? What's going on?"

Anna slumped onto a chair. Tough Cookie sashayed over, wrapped herself around Anna's ankles a few times, then jumped onto her lap. "You know I need a hug, don't you?" Anna whispered into the cat's fur. To her mother, she said, "It's just something that Evan—Patrolman Burley, you saw him the other day—told me."

"Something bad?" Her mother perched on the edge of the sofa.

Anna raised one shoulder in an awkward shrug. "Not bad, just... just something he shouldn't have told me."

"And you're being arrested for it?" Barbara jumped up.

"No, nothing like that." Anna wanted to laugh at the absurdity of the question but couldn't even break a smile. "It's okay. You can relax. I don't know what's going to happen. Evan is in some kind of trouble about it. And the other person involved—the one Evan told me about—might sue me if he thinks I'm spreading tales about him."

Barbara nodded as she walked over to the window. "I see. Well then." She turned back to Anna. "You need to stop talking about him, don't you?"

Anna blew out a deep breath. "That's about the gist of it, yes. But what about Evan?"

"He's a grown man. He can take care of himself. You need to worry about yourself, your home, and your family." She glanced out the window. "This storm is coming in soon. I need to get home, to start making these calls. Will you be okay here on your own?"

"I'm not on my own. Am I, Tough Cookie?" Anna snuggled the cat.

Tough Cookie purred loudly.

"I meant besides the cat, dear." Barbara's voice oozed false patience.

"I know what you meant. But still, I'm not alone. I'll call Luke. I'm sure he'll come over."

"Good idea. Just in case anything happens during the storm that you can't handle. Your guests are relying on you to take care of things, you know."

"I know, Mom." Anna heard the whine in her voice and bit her lip. Barbara was just trying to help. "Yes, please do go home and get started on those calls about Eoin. I can't tell you how much I appreciate you getting the ball rolling on that. I know it won't be easy." Anna slid out from under Tough Cookie and crossed the room to hug her mother.

"I'm happy to help, dear. You know I am. And I meant what I said." Barbara held Anna at arm's length to look her in the eye. "I really am impressed by what you've done with this old place, very proud."

Anna beamed at her mother's praise but jumped when a tree branch landed heavily on the porch.

"Oh dear," Barbara said. "If I'm going to go, I better go now, before the storm gets worse. But one more question."

"Yes?"

"Why are you so worried for that patrolman—Evan?"

"Why? Because he's a friend, Mom, a good friend."

Barbara raised an eyebrow. "Just a friend?"

"Yes, Mom. Just a friend. Now go, and call me when you get home. I want to know you made it back safely."

Anna kissed her mother goodbye then watched her pull out of the small parking area behind the house. Once her mom was gone, she grabbed her phone and dialed. It rang so many times on the other end she thought Luke wasn't going to answer. When he finally did pick up, his voice was hard, his words curt.

"Hi."

"Hi. Oh... um... is something wrong?"

"Wrong? No, what could possibly be wrong? I'm guessing you're calling to let me know you'll be a little late to meet me for coffee? This morning?"

"Oh no, I totally forgot!" Anna grimaced and smacked her head with her free hand. "I'm so sorry, Luke. I didn't mean to blow you off like that."

Luke's voice softened, marginally. "So, what happened? Are you okay?"

Anna laughed bitterly. "Mostly. I just had to go to the police station."

"To see Evan?" The harshness returned to Luke's voice.

"Actually, no, not to see Evan. It's about Rick." A rush of wind blew into the lounge as a group of Anna's guests came back, tamping down their windblown hair and laughing. "Look, I'm really sorry about coffee. Can you come over tonight? I'll make you dinner."

He paused, and for a moment, Anna thought Luke was going to decline her invitation. She bit her lip and waited.

"Fine, I'll be there soon. Just need to prep a few things around here for the storm."

Anna thanked him then ran out to the hall to make sure her guests were safe. Several had come back to change and get rain gear before heading out to dinner. Anna watched as they bundled up, their biggest concern being whether or not it was worth bringing an umbrella with the wind as strong as it was. Anna wished she could leave worrying about the big things to someone else too—things like whether a tree would come down on the house in a storm, if Rick Enright would sue her, and worst of all, if Evan would ever talk to her again.

"Thanks again for coming over." Anna put down the spoon she'd been using to stir the pot of tomato sauce and came to give Luke a quick hug.

"Sure," Luke replied casually, pulling away from Anna's embrace. "It means I get to spend more time with this guy." He slid his chair closer to Eoin, who looked up from his notebook and grinned. "What you got there?"

"It's my notes," Eoin responded solemnly.

"Your notes?"

Eoin nodded, his red mess of hair bouncing along with the movement. "I take notes, y'see. They're in here."

"Right, I understood that part." Luke grinned. "But notes of what?"

"Oh, everything." Again, Eoin's voice conveyed the seriousness with which he took his note-taking responsibilities.

Luke gave up trying to understand and turned to face Anna. For a moment, the sight of Luke, large, solid, reliable, sexy, having a serious conversation with little Eoin cheered her. But then he tightened his lips into a narrow frown and looked away. "So, what's going to happen next with the police report?"

Anna shrugged and walked back to the stove as the windows rattled against the storm. "I have no idea. It's all a complete disaster. I'm just waiting around to see if Rick is going to sue me. And I can't talk to Evan—"

"What do you think?" Luke cut her off as soon as she mentioned Evan, turning his attention back to Eoin.

Eoin shrugged. "I didn't like that man."

"Rick Enright?" Anna walked back over to the table. "You didn't like him?"

Eoin shook his head. "He seemed angry."

"He did, didn't he? I can't believe he just assumed Evan had told me about his record."

"But he had told you," Luke pointed out impatiently. "Maybe Rick is more astute than you give him credit for."

Anna thought about that. "Angela wouldn't have dated him if he didn't have some brains. That's true."

Luke pointed a finger at her. "Exactly. I told you before, just because the man wanted to spend more time with his girlfriend and get her away from the business that was consuming all of her time doesn't make him a killer."

Anna smiled at Luke. "At least I know you'd never try to get me away from Climbing Rose Cottage. You love this place as much as I do."

"I've put enough work into it." Luke finally smiled, his first of the evening. "I definitely do not want you to leave Climbing Rose Cottage. In fact, I want you to stay."

He put a hand out, and Anna grabbed it, grateful that he seemed to have finally forgiven her for forgetting about him earlier. She squeezed his hand tightly then dropped it when the lights flickered.

"Uh-oh. I hope we don't lose power." She shuddered as another loud gust shook the house.

Eoin's eyes opened wide. "We could light candles, like they did in the old days."

Anna laughed. "Yes, we could. But I don't know how much my guests would appreciate that."

"Don't worry." Luke ruffled Eoin's hair. "You've still got that old generator out back. I can get it up and running in no time if it comes to that. It won't be enough to power everything, but it will keep the fridge cold and the lights on."

Anna went back to stirring the sauce, trying to ignore the gale growing outside. She could picture the tall trees that lined the historic street shaking under its pressure, dark waves towering over the sand before crashing onto the beach. She only hoped the trees would stand and the water would stay down at the shoreline. At least lots of driftwood and flotsam would be on the beach tomorrow for the treasure hunters who walked up and down after any storm. She wouldn't be one of them. Her focus would be on Climbing Rose Cottage.

She pushed away thoughts of how much cleanup tomorrow might require and pulled out a box of dried pasta to boil. She'd picked up some fresh bread on her way home from the police station and put that in the oven to warm as she pulled out the tray of meatballs. "I just hope Rick doesn't sue me. I have no money, just the house."

Luke stood and came up close behind her. "Don't worry, I'll talk to him, but I really don't think you need to worry about that. Rick is a good guy. I've been telling you."

"I don't think you should talk to him." Anna turned to face Luke. "I think that would just make it worse."

Luke laughed. "I wouldn't do it if I thought it would make things worse. I'll talk to him, but you need to stop digging around in this murder. Stop sticking your nose into other people's business. That's what got you into this situation."

Anna thought again about how angry Isabelle had been. "I have been annoying a lot of people." She shook her head. "But I still think Rick reacted weirdly. He overreacted. Just because I was scared of him, he turned around and filed a complaint against me?" She stirred the sauce mindlessly. "That doesn't seem right."

Luke shrugged. "Maybe he's more sensitive than I realized. Maybe you reacted more obviously than you realized." He walked back to the table. "Since I clearly won't convince you to drop this, do you have any real evidence?"

"Real evidence?" Eoin asked.

Luke nodded. "Like proof that someone did something."

"I don't think more clues are what I need." Anna spooned the pasta sauce and meatballs into a big bowl and carried it over to the table. "I need to think about the people involved."

Luke rolled his eyes as he unrolled his napkin. "Less of the emotional stuff, more hard facts—that's what you need."

A crack of thunder sounded just overhead, and even Luke jumped a little at the sudden sound, which was far too close for comfort. Eoin slid lower in his chair.

Anna's anger rose. Luke wasn't taking her seriously. "I'm not just thinking about what I need to do next." Anna placed a bowl of spaghetti on the table. "I'm thinking about Evan too."

Luke grabbed the bowl and dumped spaghetti onto his plate. "You're worried about him?"

Anna nodded as she brought the bread over then sat. "He's in real trouble at work, and it's all my fault."

Luke shook his head. "It's not your fault. It's his own

fault. He chose to give you that information without looking into it more. You just listened. You didn't make him say it."

Anna thought about that. It would be comforting to believe, but Anna knew how guilty she felt.

"Like I said, you should drop it—or stop bugging people and start gathering real evidence."

As they ate, Anna considered her options. Eoin took the opportunity of the pause in conversation to ask Luke how combustion engines worked. He absentmindedly pulled his notebook out of his pocket and put it down on the table next to his plate.

Anna shook her head. "Let's move that somewhere safe from stray spaghetti sauce, shall we?" She placed the tattered book on the sideboard and came back to her seat. "You may be right."

"About what?" Luke looked over at her as he scooped up the last of his meal.

"I do need to stop bugging people."

"Good, glad to hear it." Luke dropped his fork onto his empty plate and picked up his napkin. "It's about time you came to your senses. Now, I better go take a quick look at that generator, just to make sure it's ready to go if we need it."

He was partly out the back door before Anna stopped him by saying, "Because I need to take time to consider the information I already have."

Luke groaned and turned back to the kitchen.

"It's all in there." Eoin pointed at his notebook.

Luke groaned again as he sank back into his chair. "Really? Look, I've told you what you need to do. If you don't want to listen to me, you're on your own." He pushed up from the table and stormed out into the wind and rain.

Anna cleared the plates away, Eoin watching her silently.

"Is Luke mad?" Eoin finally asked.

"I think he is, yes," Anna answered. "But not at you, don't worry."

"I'm not worried about me, Cousin Anna." Eoin came over and wrapped his arms around her waist. "I'm worried about you. Luke is your friend."

Anna felt tears gather in her eyes and wiped them away as she hugged Eoin back. "Yes, he is, and he still will be. Don't worry about that. Now, hand me those bowls from the table."

When Luke returned to the kitchen, the dishes had been done and the counters wiped down. He paused in the doorway, water dripping from his hair and puddling on the ground around him. Anna tossed him a dishcloth, and he wiped the drops of rain from his face and arms.

"I better get home, Anna. It's pretty bad out there. But your generator is good to go. You know how to get it started, right?"

Anna nodded. "I'll be fine. Don't worry about me."

Luke barely looked her in the eye. He kissed her chastely on the cheek then headed back out into the storm.

❧ 33 ❧

Anna carried the armload of sticks and small branches over to the pile she was building at the side of the yard then straightened and wiped hair out of her eyes with the back of her wrist. As exhausted as she was after a long night of tossing and turning under the crash of the storm, she realized how lucky she'd been. The biggest branch to come down in her yard was only a few feet long. From where she stood, she could see the disaster her unfortunate neighbors were dealing with. Just two houses up, an old tree had uprooted in the storm, falling across the road and crashing onto a car.

Eoin seemed to have slept through it all with no problem. He skipped around the porch, swiping at the wet tables and chairs with a towel. He noticed her watching him and smiled, then his gaze shifted, and he waved happily. Anna turned around to see Sammy coming in through the front gate.

"Hey, buddy!" she called to Eoin before running up to hug Anna. "How are you? I heard it was bad down here, but I didn't realize just how bad." She and Anna both stared at the fallen tree, and Sammy shook her head. "I parked on the other block to avoid that mess."

"Sammy, Sammy." Eoin ran down from the porch to throw his arms around Sammy.

"How're you doing, Eoin? I hear you're going to stick around for a while."

Eoin nodded eagerly. "You betcha! I can't wait to see my new school."

Sammy laughed. "I never thought I'd hear an eight-year-old say that. Come on. I'll help you with those tables."

Anna gathered the rest of the branches from the yard then joined Sammy and Eoin on the porch, where Sammy had just finished going back over the tables Eoin had taken swipes at. Anna grabbed one of the towels from the pile and joined them.

"Thanks for coming over, Sammy."

"Of course. I had to when I heard what happened." She stopped wiping the table and looked carefully at Anna. "You don't look so great. I'm not used to seeing you with circles under your eyes."

"Gee, thanks." Anna smiled, but it didn't keep. "I couldn't sleep. The storm, you know."

"That wasn't all that was keeping you up, though, was it? I can't believe anyone would file a complaint against you. That's ridiculous." She dropped her towel and put both hands on Anna's arms, looking her straight in the eye. "Seriously, you're the sweetest, kindest person I know. You don't deserve this. Now, do you want me to key his car or something?"

Anna laughed, grateful for the release. She could always count on Sammy. "Well, if he's the killer, then he's not exactly a rational person, is he? And I'll tell you what, if Rick didn't kill James, he's sure acting guilty. I mean, setting the police on me to get me to back off?" Anna reached for another chair, straightening it against the small table.

"The best defense is a good offense, right?" Sammy pointed out, back at work on a table with Eoin.

Eoin looked up at her with questioning eyes.

"It's a sports expression," she told him. "I'll explain it later. Do you play any sports?"

Eoin shook his head.

"Anna, you're going to need to think about things like that, like what activities Eoin will be involved in at school. Maybe soccer?" She gave Eoin a questioning look.

He shrugged and looked confused.

"You'd call it football," she said.

"Oh, I like football." Eoin grinned and nodded.

Anna could just picture Eoin running up and down a soccer field, chasing a ball. He certainly had the energy for it, if not the physique. She opened her mouth to say so, when two guests came out the front door. She dropped her towel and trotted over to wish them a good day and answer any questions they had about what they could do in Cape May. Once they'd left, she returned to Sammy and Eoin.

"How much time do you have?" Anna asked.

Sammy glanced at her watch. "Not much at all. You know I'm keeping an eye on my staff. But"—she grinned at Anna and wiggled her eyebrows—"I've put a plan into action."

"A plan?" Anna laughed. "Dare I ask?"

"Don't ask yet. Let's see how it goes first. Now, what are you going to do about this complaint?"

"That's the question of the century." Anna leaned against the table and ran her hand through Eoin's hair. He ducked his head to get away from her. "Sorry." She grinned, not sorry at all. She loved the idea that he was going to stay with her for at least a year.

"Is there any way to get Rick to back off, to withdraw his complaint?"

Anna laughed. "I suppose proving he killed James would get him to back off."

"True. Or"—Sammy snapped her fingers—"even if you prove someone else did it, that would help Angela, and maybe then he'd appreciate what you'd done and withdraw it on his own."

Anna frowned, unconvinced. "He's pretty angry at Angela. I don't see him reacting that way."

"Hmm, maybe not. But either way, he isn't going to stop you from figuring out who did it, right?"

Anna shrugged, leaning down to grab another towel.

"Want to look at my notes?" Eoin dug in his pocket and pulled out his notebook.

"I do." Sammy took the book from Eoin with gravity. "Let's see." She looked at the page Eoin pointed at. "Dean Harrison." Sammy glanced at Anna. "He owns the Renata Winery, right?"

Anna nodded. "He certainly has the knowledge to kill someone that way, and I don't know where he was that morning."

"Why are you so sure it was that morning? Maybe he rigged things up in advance."

"Maybe. But then he could have killed anyone. What if Angela had been in there stirring the wine and grabbed that meter? Or one of her employees? If someone rigged this up in advance, it means they didn't care who they killed." Anna shook her head and shuddered. "No, I don't believe that. Someone must have been there that morning. Even if they cut the ventilation line the day before, they must have placed the oxygen meter that morning, right before James went in."

"And placed it at the front of the line so that was the one he would grab."

"Exactly."

"Okay, so Dean Harrison has motive?"

"He does. Pretty strong. Against both Angela and James."

"Double motive. Killing two birds with one stone," Sammy said brightly, then her face dropped. "Sorry, that was crass. James is dead, after all. But we agree, you could still learn more about Dean."

"What about that one?" Eoin pointed at the next page.

"Corey Bowman." Sammy looked up at Anna.

"I don't see it." Anna shook her head. "I mean, he might have been mad at James but not mad enough to kill him."

"I wouldn't mind seeing him again anyway." Sammy shrugged. "He's a nice guy. In fact, he could tell us more about Isabelle and Ralph. They're still at the top of your suspect list, right?"

Another guest came out but didn't stop, so Anna simply waved. "Have a great day!" she called out then returned her attention to their conversation. "She is. And as far as I know, she's still the police's top suspect. Just because her lawyer got her out of the interrogation room doesn't mean they've dropped her as a suspect." Anna stepped toward another table then realized they'd successfully dried all the tables and chairs. They were ready for any guest who wanted to spend the morning sitting outside, sipping coffee or iced tea. She stopped and looked around, not sure what to do next.

"I'm sorry you can't talk to Evan." Sammy walked over and put a hand on Anna's arm. "I'm really sorry this is happening to you."

"Me too. It's certainly helpful having a cop on my side when I'm looking for information."

"It's not just that, though, is it?" Sammy asked.

Anna shrugged. "I guess I can talk to Ralph again. He's been helpful so far."

"He won't be helpful if he knows you're trying to finger his mother for murder!"

"No, probably not." She smiled gratefully at Sammy. "I know you have to get back, but thank you."

"For what, helping with this?" Sammy glanced around.

"For being here, when I know you have your own problems to work on." She hugged Sammy.

"Of course I'm here. Just like you're always there for me when I need you." Sammy hugged her back.

Eoin jumped over and threw his arms around both women as far as he could reach, which wasn't far. He spoke with his face against Anna's back, his voice muffled. "Beth-Anne is coming home today. I bet she'll be at the library." He released his hug to jump up and down. "Can we go, Cousin Anna? Can we? Can we?"

"Okay, okay." Anna laughed, raising both hands in capitulation. "We'll go find your new best friend."

❦ 34 ❦

Eoin skipped along the sidewalk ahead of Anna, jumping over puddles, pointing excitedly at birds perched in nearby trees. Anna couldn't help but laugh out loud, her relief tangible at his upbeat mood. It was good to see Eoin back to his normal self. Once the library came into view, Eoin ran ahead. By the time Anna was inside, he was holding BethAnne's hand, looking up at her with adoring eyes.

Felicia stood behind the counter, but her focus was on BethAnne.

"Another murder, Ms. McGregor?" BethAnne asked as Anna approached.

"I know. I don't like it either," Anna replied with concern. A difficult experience a couple of months earlier had caused BethAnne's parents to take her out of town for a few weeks. It couldn't be welcome news to come home to. "I'm so glad to see you back in town. How are you?"

BethAnne shrugged and smiled. "I'm fine, really. I kept telling my parents that. They had nothing to worry about."

Felicia glanced at Anna and shook her head quickly, as if

to say, "Don't ask." "The resilience of youth," she said, "a truly wonderful thing."

"I'm glad you're back too," Eoin said, his voice taut as he kept his head turned up, his eyes trained on BethAnne.

BethAnne laughed and hugged him. "And I'm so glad you'll be sticking around for a while."

Eoin's eyes lit up. "Will we be in the same school?"

BethAnne scrunched up her face. "I'm afraid not. I go to the high school."

Eoin's expression fell, and he looked down.

"But I'll still see you all the time. We'll still be friends, right?"

Eoin grinned and nodded, taking BethAnne's hand again. "Someday we'll be old friends, just like Cousin Anna and Sammy."

Felicia cleared her throat and brought the conversation back to a more serious topic. "Before you came in, I was explaining how James Longhurst died at the White Pine Winery."

BethAnne nodded. "I know a little bit about the chemistry of it, not much."

"It's kind of scary," Anna said. "Carbon dioxide poisoning. It's something all winemakers are aware of and take steps to control. It's terrible that it happened at Angela's winery."

"It's hard to understand how it could've happened." BethAnne wrinkled her brow. "If more than three percent of the air we breathe is carbon dioxide, we start feeling dizzy."

Anna put an approving hand on her shoulder. "And if that goes as high as seven percent, things get dangerous. That can cause someone to fall unconscious within a few minutes."

"A few minutes?" Felicia asked.

Anna nodded. "That's all it would take."

"Who would do such a thing?" BethAnne wondered aloud.

Felicia mumbled something as she turned her attention to the pile of books on her desk.

"What was that?" Anna leaned forward.

"Oh, just that gossip is sometimes wrong." Felicia let out a sigh and leaned both elbows on the counter. "I talked to my friend Michelle again."

"The one who saw Dean at White Pine Winery on Monday morning?"

Felicia nodded. "That's the one. Now she's not so sure it was Dean. She says she glimpsed him turning into the parking lot from a distance. She was driving the other direction, so she only saw him for a second."

"So maybe Dean wasn't at the winery that morning," Anna said thoughtfully. "But that doesn't prove anything, does it? Maybe he was who Michelle saw. Maybe he wasn't, but he still could have been there."

"Or not," Felicia pointed out.

Anna chewed her lip, thinking.

"What're you talking about?" BethAnne finally asked.

"Another winemaker, dear," Felicia explained. "Someone thought they'd seen him at White Pine Winery that morning, but it might not have been him."

"What else can you tell me about Dean?" Anna asked Felicia. "What about that meeting with Anthony Middleton?"

"Aha, that I can look up." Felicia turned to her computer and tapped on the keyboard.

"You can look up information about their meeting?" Anna asked skeptically.

"No, of course not," Felicia said. "But I can tell you more about Anthony. Let's see... yes, here we are."

Felicia turned the monitor so the others could see what she was looking at—all of them except Eoin, who couldn't see over the top of the counter. After a couple of hops, he ran around to stand next to Felicia instead.

"He's in real estate? With a specialty in agricultural land?" Anna asked, confused. "Do you think Dean is selling his winery?"

"Not a chance." Felicia let out a gentle laugh. "Buying, more likely."

Anna's eyes opened wide. "Buying Angela's winery, you mean?"

Felicia raised an eyebrow. "Makes sense, doesn't it?"

"Oh, that's terrible." Anna took a step back from the counter, as if separating herself from it would distance her from the idea. "Would he do something so horrible just so Angela would sell her winery to him?" She turned to pace along the edge of the counter. "Ugh, this is so frustrating."

"What is, dear?"

"Not being able to talk to Evan about this."

"Why can't you?" BethAnne asked. "This is a good lead. You should tell him."

Anna felt herself blush and waved a hand in embarrassment. "You're right, of course. So, when Dean heard James was going to be there that afternoon, he popped in, cut the cable, and recalibrated the meter at the front of the line, knowing James would simply take the first one."

"Why did he need to kill James?" BethAnne asked. "If he just wanted to put the winery out of business, it could have been anyone."

"It's probably worth talking this through with Evan," Felicia said.

"I'm sure Evan wouldn't appreciate my getting in the way. He knows how to do his job." Anna looked down.

Felicia raised an eyebrow. "Anna, you know he appreciates your help. Tell me, what's going on?"

"Oh, Felicia, I did something terrible, and now Evan isn't talking to me."

"What did you do?"

"I somehow convinced Evan it was okay for him to share confidential police records with me."

"Why did you do that?"

"I didn't mean to. He had the information. I was asking him questions. He just told me. Anyway, Detective Walsh found out. Now Evan is being disciplined, I might be sued, and Evan isn't talking to me."

Felicia looked at her. "I'm so sorry, Anna. I know how close you two are. And it's too bad you can't share notes about the case."

"Who cares about the case? I just miss talking to Evan." Anna shrugged. "Because he's Evan."

Both women fell silent, Anna staring at the ground, Felicia nodding knowingly.

Eoin had been watching the two women as they spoke, and he coughed. "So, who could have done it?"

"Besides Angela, another person was there that afternoon. Maybe Corey saw Dean. I need to talk to James's old friend again."

"Come in, come in. Good to see you." Corey greeted Anna like an old friend. His cool, quiet house felt great after the humidity of her bike ride over. The care he took of his home, inside and out, struck her once again. "Can I offer you a cup of tea?"

"That sounds fabulous, thank you." She sat in one of the elegant chairs, finding it more comfortable than it looked. When Corey returned with a tea tray, Anna jumped up to take it from him. Placing it carefully on the coffee table, she handed him his cup before taking her own. "Looks like you didn't suffer too much from last night's storm."

Corey closed his eyes as he shook his head. "Thank goodness. I can hear a few generators running on the next street, but I was lucky. Still have power. Still have a roof." He laughed, but his expression was serious. "I'd hate to lose this house."

Anna looked around the room, admiring the artwork, which she was sure was authentic and valuable.

Corey followed her gaze. "The last few remnants of my previous life. They are beautiful, aren't they?"

Anna nodded as she held her tea. "I don't know much about art, I'm afraid."

"That's quite all right. You don't need to know much to admire it. Though I admit, the more I know, the more impressed I am by the accomplishments of some of these artists." Corey lowered himself carefully onto a chair, his teacup on the mahogany table at his elbow.

"Was this collection in your family for long?" Anna asked.

Corey shook his head. "Not generations or anything like that. My mother was the art buff. She started collecting before I was born. At first, it was just an interest—an investment as well, which was why my father went along with it. But eventually, she became involved in the art community. She took classes in art appreciation—actually, now that I think about it, Isabelle Longhurst joined her in those classes. I believe my mother got Isabelle interested in artwork as well. I know they have a valuable collection at their house."

"Really?" Anna thought about that as she blew on her tea and took a sip. Definitely Earl Grey, she thought, recognizing the hint of bergamot. She let the flavor linger before asking, "How valuable?"

Corey chuckled. "I couldn't say. I don't know exactly what they have. But I can tell you that although I've held onto as much of my mother's collection as I could, I have had to sell a couple of pieces. To cover bills, you know."

Anna nodded, waiting for him to continue.

"If I sold what I have left, I could move out of this house, buy a mansion in Stone Harbor, and live comfortably there for the rest of my life with no worries." He shrugged and shook his head as he took a sip of his tea.

Is he missing his previous lifestyle or regretting its decadence? Anna wondered. She had seen the luxury Isabelle surrounded herself with, so the fact that she owned a valuable art collection came as no surprise. "Did James Longhurst appreciate the art his wife collected?"

"Ha! Hardly." Corey scoffed. "James was not always kind to Isabelle. Their relationship wasn't the best."

"In what way?"

"They started out well. At least it seemed so to me. But that didn't last long. Just a few years into their marriage, they began picking on each other. Not long after Ralph was born, in fact."

"They picked on each other?" Anna laughed. "Sounds like children."

Corey finished his tea and replaced his cup carefully on the end table, putting his left hand over his right when it started to shake. "It's true. They acted like children sometimes. He complained about her art collection, among other things. He didn't share her sense of what was beautiful."

"Modern art can be hard for some people to enjoy," Anna pointed out, looking around the room again. She didn't know whether Corey's collection counted as modern or not. It certainly looked contemporary but not the sort of geometric blocks of solid color or splashes of paint she expected from late-twentieth-century artists.

"True." Corey dipped his head in agreement. "She, meanwhile, hated his interest in wine. I think she was happier when he was spending eighty hours a week working. Once he retired, he spent a lot more time at home. And instead of coming up with a hobby, like golf, that would have taken him out of the house, he developed his wine business."

"Didn't that take his time?"

"It did, but he worked from home, so he was always underfoot. I just remember them bickering—him complaining about her spending money, her complaining about his bottles and boxes stacked in odd places."

"I would've thought he'd at least appreciate her artwork as an investment."

"I think he did, you know. I think he just enjoyed arguing with her."

Anna stood and walked over to examine one of Corey's pieces. It depicted a group of birds taking flight from a marsh, but other than the topic, it had nothing in common with popular beach art. The birds, sandhill cranes, were painted in a blue so dark it was almost black yet at the same time bright, jumping off the canvas. The near blackness of their bodies contrasted with the gray-and-white sky behind them, depicted through geometric figures. The somberness of the birds, the sky, and even the cattails they flew out of contrasted with a few bright spots of color—a tuft of red on each bird's head, a dash of yellow and green that hinted at the water below. So simple, yet so powerful. She could only guess what a painting like that was worth. She moved on to examine another when Corey interrupted her.

"There's more," he said. "Isabelle always resented that Ralph got into the wine business."

"Why?" She dragged her attention away from the artwork and turned back to her host.

Corey shrugged. "It was a competition between those two."

"For what?"

"For everything. Who had more friends, who seemed happier, and definitely who had more of Ralph's affections. When he told his parents he was using his business degree to open a wine distribution business, Isabelle threw a fit."

Anna laughed, but Corey didn't. He shook his head. "It was sad. Really it was."

"Childish."

"Yes, but even more than that. I was friendly with Ralph, too, you see, so I knew the truth. He wanted to impress his father. That was why he got into the business. But all along, all the time, he loved his mother more. I don't know why she can't see that."

"Did he get along with his father?"

"He did. To a point. Ralph hated the way his father treated his mother, laughing at her choices, picking on her for not being bright enough. He's very protective of his mother, you know. He was the one who encouraged her to take various classes, improve herself, that sort of thing."

Anna thought about Ralph's reaction when Anna had started suspecting Isabelle of the murder. "That makes sense. And it gives me something to think about." Anna reached for the tea tray, intending to carry it back to the kitchen, but Corey stopped her.

"No, no, I'll get that."

She glanced at his shaking hands but kept her mouth shut. The man clearly preferred to maintain his dignity. She nodded. "Thank you so much for your time. You've given me a lot to think about."

"Where will your investigation take you next?"

"Back to the winery. But I need to make amends with a friend first and ask for his help."

$\maltese$ 36 $\maltese$

The parking lot in front of White Pine Winery, intended for guests and patrons, held only police vehicles today. They clustered together near the door of the main shop, reminding Anna a bit of the cranes in Corey's painting—ready to take off at any minute. A large puddle had formed in the middle of the lot, so Luke parked his truck on the far side. As they walked toward the entrance, he placed a protective hand on her shoulder. She put her hand over his but kept her face turned away from him.

He'd taken her apology well. She'd explained that she was going to take his advice and find more "real" evidence back at the winery. In response, he'd simply asked how he could help. Thinking about it, she squeezed his hand and looked up at him. *Why does accepting his advice make me so mad?* He grinned back down at her, and she felt the usual flutter in her stomach.

He dropped her hand as he pulled open the winery door and ushered her in ahead of him. The storefront was empty, but they found Angela in her back office, packing up supplies.

She greeted them with a frown and a shake of her head. "It's good to see you, Anna. What a mess." She waved a hand vaguely to capture the room.

"Don't be in too much of a hurry to pack up, Angela. You know I'm still working on this."

"Any new clues?" Angela perked up a little.

"Well..." Anna glanced at Luke. "I wouldn't say clues, exactly. More like theories."

Luke laughed gently under his breath. "How'd the winery hold up in the storm, Angela?"

"Not bad, all things considered. A couple of branches down beyond the grapes, but only a few broken vines. I'm lucky, considering the grapes are so heavy right now. Oh." She looked away for a moment. "What am I saying? They won't be my grapes to harvest, will they?"

"Speaking of that," Anna said, jumping in, "is it possible someone might have sneaked in on Monday and you didn't notice? Someone like, oh... maybe Dean Harrison?"

"Dean? I'm pretty sure I would have noticed Dean poking around."

"How many ways are there to get in?" Anna asked.

"Come on. I'll show you." Angela led them through to the barn, pointing out the small door on the far side and the wide double doors that led to the patio. A cluster of men and women in working clothes huddled just outside that door, talking with a uniformed officer.

"He—or whoever," Anna added, just to be cautious, "could have come in through the tasting room and shop too."

Angela shook her head. "I would have seen them."

"So it must have been someone who knows the place

and who your staff would recognize and not question," Anna said.

"Didn't the police question the staff to see if they saw anyone?" Luke asked, surprised.

"I believe that's what they're doing right now." Angela indicated the group on the patio.

Just then, Evan came in through the double doors. He must have been talking to someone outside beyond their vision. Anna's sharp inhalation caught Evan's attention. His eyes softened, and a smile started to form on his lips, then he shook his head as if reminding himself. He looked away from her, turning to Luke instead. Anna sighed. She couldn't blame him. He'd been told specifically not to talk to her, and he had every reason to play things by the book.

"Hey, bud, I wanted to tell you." Luke put a hand on Evan's arm. "I talked to Rick. He's not going to pursue his complaint. I know you're still dealing with the fallout and all, but at least it won't get any worse."

"What complaint?" Angela asked. "Rick filed a complaint against Evan?"

"It was because of me, but Evan got in trouble. And Rick threatened to sue me too." Anna added.

"How could he? You're my friends. You're involved because I asked for your help."

Anna shrugged and looked at her feet. "It's possible things might have gotten a little out of hand. I learned some things I shouldn't have—things that turned out not to be true."

Angela threw her arms out in frustration. "Oh no! I should have told you more about Rick myself. He's selfish, true, but he's gentle, kind. He wouldn't hurt anyone."

Anna sneaked a glance at Evan. He wouldn't meet her eyes, his anger at himself for what he did showing on his face.

"All right, let's go look at the scene of the crime again, right?" Luke asked brightly.

Angela led Luke into the tank room, Anna close on their heels, Evan slightly farther behind.

"Take a breath," Angela said when Anna stepped into the room. "Smell that?"

Anna took a deep breath. "Hmm, I don't smell a whole lot. Sort of yeasty, I guess? Almost like beer but fruitier." Anna shrugged apologetically. "But to be honest, I don't smell much."

"Exactly. That's because the air circulation is working properly. I would notice immediately if it weren't, before it got to a dangerous stage, because I know the air in here. I walk in and take a breath right away. It's natural for me."

"And the meters?"

Angela gestured to where they were lined up in a row on a shelf. "Anyone coming in would naturally grab the first one. Why dig around behind it for a different one?"

"But if the killer didn't care who they killed, then they could have stuck the incorrectly calibrated meter in the middle and just waited until someone picked it up," Anna pointed out.

"I guess that's possible." Angela frowned. "But who would do that? Kill someone randomly, I mean."

"They might not have intended for the victim to die," Anna said.

Evan shook his head. "I don't buy it. I think whoever did this was here that morning or early afternoon. It was someone who knew James well enough to know he would come in here to stir the wine. They cut the line and dropped the faulty meter in the front row."

"Anyone who knew James would know he'd come in here," Angela said. "That was hardly a secret. He loved wine. He came in here every time he visited the winery. I'm sure he did the same thing at the other wineries too."

"So someone like Dean Harrison would know," Anna pointed out.

"True."

Anna chewed on her lip. She needed to get away from it for a while, to think about what she already knew. She walked over to the vat and put a hand on it. It was only a few inches taller than she was, with a ladder running up one side. She glanced at Luke, who was watching her closely.

"Angela, can I go up there? Where James was?"

Luke stepped forward. "Why? You know it's dangerous."

Angela shook her head. "It's really not dangerous. I can tell you the air is fine. Just don't stir the wine." She gave Anna a look of warning.

"I won't, I promise."

"Then it's perfectly safe." Angela gestured toward the ladder that ran up the side of the tank.

Anna put a foot on the ladder, shook it to confirm it was locked in place, and climbed up. One step was all she needed to see the top of the vat. Two more steps, and she was at a height where she could just about use the paddle to stir the wine—except that there was a lid covering the top of the vat. "Tell me again how this works."

Angela came closer. "He simply had to remove the lid. It comes right off." She demonstrated by lifting the lid slightly. "I usually have one of my workers help with sliding this off, but I'm sure James could have done it himself. Then he would simply grab the stirring rod, climb up a few steps, and stir."

Anna climbed up one more step. At that level, her knees brushed against the top of the vat. She glanced around the room to see what else she could see. Luke moved away from the group and walked over to reexamine the compartment that hid the cut wire, poking around to see what else he could find. Anna stood a little taller to see what Luke was doing, following him with her eyes. When he ducked into the compartment, she shifted back on the ladder to see more.

A little too far back.

She lost her balance, her arms windmilling around as she tried to regain it. But it was too late. Her arms continued to flail for the second she was in the air then landed solidly around Evan's neck.

"I've got you," he said in her ear.

And he did. He'd caught her as she fell, like something out of a movie. Anna stayed perfectly still for a moment, realizing how strong Evan's arms felt around her, how safe she felt as he held her.

Luke trotted over. "Are you okay?"

She nodded as she slipped from Evan's arms. "I'm fine, thank you. It wasn't that high, just a few steps up the ladder."

"That's it. I'm taking down that ladder. That vat must be cursed or something." Angela grabbed the ladder as she spoke, shaking it to pull it loose from the tank as Luke grabbed Anna's hand.

"Come on. We better get out of here before you hurt yourself."

Anna laughed awkwardly, but her mind was in turmoil. She needed to talk to Sammy.

"Thanks for coming with me." Anna glanced at Sammy behind the wheel.

"Coming with you or taking you?" Sammy grinned. "You know I love helping, and the bakery is closed for the day. Plus, I don't see you riding your bike up here. But why didn't Luke take you?"

Anna shook her head. "He said he had other work he needed to do. But I suspect he thinks I need to stop sticking my nose into other people's business and bugging them."

"Hmph, what does he know?" Sammy looked at Anna out of the corner of her eye. "Of course, he might have a point."

"I know, I know. It's getting really frustrating, though."

"What is?"

Anna shrugged. "I wish he'd be more supportive. Instead, he just keeps telling me what to do."

"Isn't that his way of being supportive?" Sammy pointed out. "He wants to help, so he's making helpful suggestions."

Anna rolled her eyes. "Well, when you put it that way, of course he is. Then the question is, why does it bother me so much?" She looked at her friend. "Am I really that unreasonable?"

"Don't make me answer that." Sammy laughed. "Look, you know what you want, and that's a good thing. I give you advice all the time. It doesn't seem to bother you."

"Sometimes I even follow it," Anna added with a laugh.

"Right. So if Luke trying to offer his advice bothers you, then maybe that's a sign of a bigger problem." Sammy paused then added. "Have you spoken with Evan?"

Heat rose in Anna's face as she thought of Evan, and she turned toward the window so Sammy wouldn't notice. "Kind of. He was at the winery. He... uh... he helped me when I tripped over something."

Sammy didn't respond, though Anna could guess her friend's thoughts. They were heading north out of Cape May toward Cape May Courthouse, the county seat a few miles up the parkway. After a couple of stoplights, the highway split, a wide, wooded area separating the northbound and southbound lanes. Anna looked out her window as they drove by the marshes between the Wildwoods and the parkway. An egret waded there, keeping his gaze firmly on the water, his eyes on the prize.

"It's funny," Anna said. "I have this idea I want to check out. But on the other hand, I have this lingering question about who was really targeted here. I feel like I don't have my head in the game."

"Um, I think it's safe to say James Longhurst was the victim."

"Right, obviously. But did the killer mean to kill James or intend just to hurt someone, anyone, and put Angela out of business?"

"Wow." Sammy blew out a loud breath. "That would be truly cold-blooded." She shook her head, her eyes on the road. "Okay, so, what if the target was Angela?"

"Rick is a definite possibility for the killer, then." Anna shuddered. "Not only was his reaction to my questioning way too aggressive, he has motive and means and probably opportunity. But I don't know..." Her voice trailed off as she turned her gaze back to the marshlands.

"It's a stretch, isn't it? To think that he wanted Angela out of that winery so badly he was willing to kill someone to get it?"

"Exactly."

"Then there's Dean Harrison. He clearly had the means, and it turns out he doesn't have an alibi, since Ralph wasn't with him. Plus, he has more motive than I realized."

"How so?"

"He was seen in town meeting with a realtor," Anna said, a note of triumph in her voice.

"A realtor?" Sammy's flat tone cut Anna back down to reality.

"Well, yeah. I know I'm filling in a lot of blanks here, but what if he wants to buy Angela's winery? A tragic accident forces her to shut down. She decides to sell, and look who's there to snatch it up?"

"Filling in blanks?" Sammy laughed. "It kinda sounds like you're filling in the whole picture. Why shouldn't Dean be meeting with a realtor? Do you know where he lives or if he's moving?"

"Hmm, no."

Sammy pulled onto the exit ramp, stopping at the end as she waited for an opportunity to make a left turn. The ding of a text message brought a smile to her face.

"Do you need to see what that was?" Anna asked. She

tried to keep her curiosity in check, but she couldn't conceal her concern for her friend.

Sammy shook her head. "Not while I'm driving, you know that. I'll check when we get there. But I have an idea." She pulled into a break in the traffic, passed under the parkway, and turned right onto Route 9. "And please don't worry." She glanced quickly at Anna. "I've got things under control. I think."

Cape May Courthouse didn't look anything like Cape May. Only fifteen minutes away by car, it was open, more rural. The houses and businesses along the road were well spaced, power lines tracking along both sides of the wide road. As they drove into town, restaurants and stores cropped up here and there. Anna knew the main street would have people out walking, a couple of outdoor cafes, typical life in a classic South Jersey town. But they weren't going that far. They kept their eyes on the road, looking for the sign.

"That's the thing, though, isn't it?" Anna picked up where their conversation had dropped off. "If Dean doesn't have an alibi, Ralph doesn't either. And the winery staff wouldn't blink an eye if they saw him walking around. They might not even think to tell the police, since he's such a normal face to see there."

"But why? Did he just hate his dad and want to kill him despite not benefitting from his death? That's evil. Someone like that—you'd think you'd see it in their eyes or something, you know?"

"I know. I can't figure that out. Look, there it is." Anna pointed at a small sign almost hidden by the trees.

From the outside, the Longhurst Distribution Center looked like a nineteenth-century factory. A red brick building, its main facade almost looked like a school, but wings going back from the front section of the building had been modernized.

"We're here. Let's go look Ralph in the eye and see what we see."

38

"Not you again." Isabelle closed her eyes as if praying for patience. She'd been pacing Ralph's office when they arrived and now sank into one of two plastic chairs in front of the metal desk. "I'm not sure how much more of this I can take, Ralph."

Anna glanced at Sammy, intending to share a smile at Isabelle's histrionics, but Sammy was focused on her phone.

"I'll take care of them, Mother. You just wait here." Ralph nodded to Anna and Sammy, who followed him out of the sparse workplace.

The office opened straight into the main warehouse, a vast space that looked the length of a football field and was equally wide. They walked past rows of metal shelving stretching halfway up to the lofty ceiling and spaced wide enough to allow a small forklift to drive between them.

"I am sorry for what you and your mother are going through," Anna said as she caught up to Ralph, who had taken up a brisk pace. "I can only imagine what it's like to have your father murdered."

"And be suspected of doing it." Sammy nodded.

Ralph glanced at Sammy with a raised eyebrow. "Yeah, it's not good. Now, why are you here? What can I do for you?"

"Actually, we just wanted to see where you work and how you work, to see this warehouse." Anna felt that was a sufficient explanation. She didn't need to tell him they wanted to look him in the eye and see if he was a murderer.

Sammy walked on Ralph's other side, occasionally glancing at his face. He gave her another odd look and moved away from her. When he looked away, Sammy took the opportunity to shrug at Anna and shake her head. No clues from Ralph's eyes, then.

Anna rubbed her hands along her arms. "It's not very warm in here."

"It's temperature controlled, of course," Ralph replied. "Best temperature for wine storage is fifty-six degrees. A bit of a challenge this morning, of course."

"Why's that?"

"The storm, you know? We lost power for a while. That was rough." Ralph pointed at a series of cables that ran out through a narrow gap from a propped door. "I have a series of generators out there, but they don't generate enough power to keep this place cool."

"What did you do?" Sammy asked as she finished typing out yet another text message then tucked her phone back into her pocket.

Ralph scoffed. "Hoped and prayed—and bugged the heck out of the power company. And of course we have temporary structures we put up to capture cool air where we need it most."

Anna's phone vibrated just as a forklift came out from a row ahead of them. They stepped out of the way, watching as the driver expertly maneuvered the vehicle and its cargo to the loading bays along the back wall, which were neatly tucked away so the neighbors wouldn't have to see the trucks loading and unloading.

"Luke," Anna answered her phone, keeping her voice low and her face turned away from Ralph. "I can't talk now."

"Hot on the case, huh?" Luke sounded resigned. "Okay, but I do need to talk to you. Can I come by later?"

"Sure, that would be great," Anna replied, not thinking about her schedule or when she would be home. "Drop by anytime." She'd already returned her attention to Ralph before hanging up.

"I'm surprised by how big this place is. It didn't look this big from the outside," Sammy observed.

"One hundred thousand square feet of storage space." Ralph crossed his arms in front of his chest as he surveyed the warehouse. "We're not the largest distributor in New Jersey, not by a long shot, but we offer quality service at a reasonable price for any importer who wants to work with us."

"Why in South Jersey?" Anna asked. "I'm surprised you don't want to be closer to the airport."

"Actually, many of my clients rely on the Atlantic City International Airport. It's smaller, so it's easier to work with for the smaller loads, which my clients have. Come on." Anna and Sammy trotted along with Ralph, who kept up a surprisingly energetic speed around one row of shelving then back toward the office. "As I said, the whole space is climate controlled—the best environment for wine storage, no matter how temporary—and our distribution trucks are also temperature controlled, of course. My trucks pick up the delivery from the airport and store it here. Then we arrange deliveries to the wine retailers around the region, and the trucks take the deliveries to the retailers—"

"Ralph, are you ready yet?" Isabelle cut off Ralph's monologue, her voice carrying through the warehouse. "I'm starving."

"It's not even five o'clock, Mother," Ralph called back as he jogged toward her. "Showing her age, isn't she, ready to eat dinner at five?" He asked the question of Anna, who jogged along next to him.

Isabelle marched over to intercept them. "If you expect me to pay—which he does," she added to Anna and Sammy, "then you'll eat on my schedule."

Ralph turned bright red. "Well, there you have it. I'm afraid the tour is over, ladies." He escorted them back to the main office. "Give me a moment, Mother," he said as he stepped out again.

Left alone in the office with Isabelle, Anna tried to look casual as she sauntered over to the low shelving behind the desk, scanning the books and folders. For what, she couldn't say, but it didn't hurt to know what Ralph was up to. Isabelle didn't seem to care, focusing instead on digging through her purse. Anna's gaze ran over a stack of manila file folders then jumped back as she recognized the bright-yellow plastic sticking out from behind the pile. She nudged Sammy and pointed at it. Isabelle finally realized something had happened and turned to see what they were looking at.

"Do you know what that is?" Anna asked Isabelle, nudging the folders to the side so the oxygen meter was almost fully exposed.

Isabelle shrugged. "Ralph has all kinds of equipment around here. You heard him bragging about his warehouse space. Climate control—temperature, humidity, blah blah blah. I'm sure he has meters to measure everything from the amount of oxygen in the air to the number of aliens who have landed." She snorted at her own joke then raised her hand to cover her mouth at the inelegant sound.

Sammy gave Anna a look, and Anna agreed. *It might be that Ralph required an oxygen meter in his work—but the exact same make and model as Angela's?* That was quite a coincidence.

Ralph returned. "Okay, Mother, I'm ready."

"Finally." Isabelle gathered her purse and a silk wrap just as the front door banged open. Detective Walsh and Evan strode in.

"Isabelle Longhurst?" Walsh asked.

Isabelle rolled her eyes again. "You know perfectly well it's me. What do you want now? In fact." She reached into her purse and pulled out her phone. "I'm calling my lawyer."

"You can do that from the station, ma'am. I'm placing you under arrest."

"You're what?"

"You can't do that!" Ralph spluttered.

"Please turn around, ma'am."

"You're handcuffing me?" She tossed her purse and phone to Ralph, who caught them awkwardly.

"You can't do that to my mother," Ralph babbled as Walsh read Isabelle her rights and clipped the handcuffs around her wrists. "This is ridiculous."

"Call my lawyer, Ralph, now!"

Ralph nodded and fumbled for the phone, which slipped through his fingers and slid under the desk. He groaned but got down on his hands and knees to dig the phone out.

Anna nudged Evan, who glanced at her but made a face that clearly said, "Not right now." She nudged him again and pointed at the bright-yellow oxygen meter. Evan's eyes opened wider, a flicker of recognition passing through them. He moved as if to say something to Walsh, but Walsh was already escorting Isabelle out to the waiting patrol car.

"Sorry," Evan whispered. "I have to go. I'll let Walsh know it's there. Take a picture of it, too, just in case."

He stopped speaking as Ralph came up from under the desk. Evan jogged out to the waiting car. Ralph was already tapping on Isabelle's phone as he walked out to his own car. Anna and Sammy shared a look as Anna pulled out her own phone to take a picture. She snapped the meter from a few different angles.

"Here, try this." Sammy grabbed a newspaper from the desk and held it up with the date clearly visible.

"It's not a kidnapping, Sammy. This isn't proof of life."

"I don't know. It kind of is."

"But the pictures are already date-stamped."

"Oh, good point. Do they record location?"

Anna nodded.

"Hmm. Okay, try this, then." Using the newspaper, Sammy pushed the other files fully away from the meter to give Anna a better view. After a few more shots, Sammy used the newspaper to flip the meter onto its other side.

"What are you doing? That's evidence."

"I didn't touch it. You saw that. But this way you can get more pictures of it." When Anna hesitated and glanced at the door, Sammy turned toward her, hands on her hips. "You heard Evan. He might not be back to get this. And that would give Ralph plenty of time to get rid of it, right? We need to get as many pictures—from as many angles—as we can now."

Anna let out a frustrated breath. "Of course, you're right." Anna walked right up to the meter, leaning forward as she snapped pictures from every possible angle, using the newspaper to shift the meter just as Sammy had done.

"Anna?"

She jumped back at the sound of Evan's voice. He looked questioningly at her then at the meter. "Did you touch it?"

"No, I promise, neither of us did." Anna stepped back, giving Evan plenty of room to collect the evidence.

"I seriously hope not. You know we're going to test this for prints. If yours are on it..." He let the sentence drift away as he shook his head.

"Evan! What do you take me for?" Anna's anger rose. He was the one who'd screwed up by telling her confidential information. She didn't deserve to be treated like an idiot.

"All right, sorry. I'll take this back to the station. Come on. You better get out of here."

Anna and Sammy led the way back to the parking lot, Evan close behind. As soon as they were outside, Evan trotted over to his car without another glance at Anna.

❧ 39 ❧

"What does it mean?" Anna leaned forward on the sofa, her chin in her hands, her elbows on her knees, staring at the pictures she'd pulled up on her laptop, which sat in the middle of the coffee table. "What does it tell us?"

Eoin, seated on the floor next to the coffee table, leaned forward too. With his face only inches from the screen, he used the mouse to flip through a few images then sat back onto his haunches and scribbled in his notebook.

"I guess it tells us..." Sammy, sitting on the floor next to Eoin, paused and screwed up her lips. "Well, it tells us that Ralph was doing something with this meter, right?"

Anna tipped her head to one side. "Assuming he knew it was there. What if it was planted?"

Eoin nodded rapidly and jotted more notes.

"What, exactly, is it?"

Luke's voice from the doorway startled them all. Eoin's pencil slipped in his fingers. Sammy twisted her head to look, and Anna jumped up.

"Oh, Luke, I didn't hear you come in."

"No, you were pretty focused on that." He pointed at the laptop. "So, what are you looking at?"

Anna grabbed her phone, pulled up the pictures, and tossed it to Luke. "It's an oxygen meter, just like the ones Angela uses. We found it in Ralph's warehouse and took pictures of it."

Luke raised an eyebrow as he swiped through a few images. "I'm glad you only took pictures, not the actual meter."

Anna balled her hands into fists at her sides. "Why do people keep assuming I'm going to do something that stupid?"

"Okay, I'm sorry. Calm down." Luke held up his hands in defense. "You're right. I know you're smarter than that. I apologize."

Anna huffed out a breath and sat back down, trying to focus on the image in front of her. A series of scratches stood out on the back of the meter, right around the spot where the front and back halves of the plastic device fit tightly together.

Luke came to stand next to her, looking at the image with her. "Someone's definitely been messing with that." He ran a finger along the scratches then clicked through a few more images, each showing the damage from a different angle. "It looks like they were trying to pry it open."

"Maybe they succeeded. Who knows?" Anna said. "But the question is, why?"

"To mess it up," Sammy said. "We know someone tampered with Angela's oxygen meters."

"But just the one that James used," Anna pointed out. "Evan said the rest of them were fine."

Anna stared at the screen, chewing on her lip, as Luke leaned forward to click through more images. Eoin settled back onto his heels and dug through his notebook, his eyes scanning the pages closely. Sammy sat back and watched, her eyes moving between the screen, Anna, and Luke.

"Luke," Sammy finally said, "did you want—"

"Practice!" Eoin shouted, waving his book and interrupting Sammy.

"Eoin, Sammy was talking," Anna chided.

"It's okay, don't worry." Sammy waved a hand. "What do you mean 'practice'?"

"Remember when I learned those cool science tricks with Felicia?" Eoin asked eagerly, watching Anna.

"Sure, you took your fingerprint and wrote secret messages."

"But I didn't do it right the first time." He looked down at his book and mumbled, "Or the second time." He looked back up at the adults, grinning. "First I used too much lemon juice. Then I smeared my fingerprint."

Anna leaned over to put a hand on Eoin's shoulder. "But you were great at it, eventually. Felicia said you learned quickly."

"I know, Cousin Anna. That's not it."

"So, what is it?" Sammy leaned forward too.

Even Luke sat down on the sofa next to Anna to be closer to Eoin's level.

The boy looked around the room triumphantly. "That's his practice, see? Like the pieces of paper I had to throw away at Felicia's. He didn't know how to do it, so he had to practice."

"Phew." Luke blew out a breath. "The boy is a genius, isn't he?"

Eoin basked in the praise as Anna nodded. "Eoin, you must be right. Ralph got the same kind of meter that Angela uses and messed with it in the privacy of his warehouse." Anna thought for a moment longer then added, "I bet he got more than one. Once he got one working the way he wanted, he just needed to drop it at the front of the line at Angela's. No one would notice one extra."

"That seems like a bit of a stretch," Sammy said. "How could he know exactly what kind? What if the color was off a little?"

Anna shrugged. "He was there often enough. He would have seen them."

"Plus, Isabelle was in the office alone. What if she planted it?" Sammy asked, sticking another dagger in Anna's growing theory.

"Technically, anyone could have put it there," Luke added.

"Isabelle?" Anna asked skeptically. "To frame her son?"

"I could see it. She's been acting weird since James died."

"I guess that's true," Anna agreed reluctantly.

"Why do you think Ralph bought new ones?" Luke asked. "He could have just taken it from Angela's. Why buy new when you can swipe a used one?"

"Hmm." Anna lowered her brows. "Angela didn't mention any being stolen. You'd think she would notice that."

"Things have been a little hectic for her recently," Sammy pointed out. She stood and stretched, reaching her arms toward the ceiling. As she did so, the lamp in the corner flickered off then on again. Sammy jumped and lowered her arms. "Did I do that?"

Anna laughed but jumped up, too, to look at the lamp. "I don't think so. But something did." She bent to look under the lampshade, its dangling fringes tickling her cheeks. "It's on now." She shook the base, and the light flickered again.

"Is that because of the storm?" Sammy asked.

"Unlikely." Luke walked over to examine the lamp, speaking as he bent down. "So, what does that tell you? About the oxygen meter, I mean."

"It means someone had to practice messing up Angela's oxygen meter enough that it wouldn't work right when James used it. Whoever it was didn't know how to recalibrate it right away. They had to learn," Sammy explained.

"We need to talk to Evan." Anna straightened.

Luke put a hand on Anna's arm. "Anna, we really need to talk. That was why I came over."

"Talk? Now?" Anna shook her head. "Can't it wait?"

Luke looked down at his hands. Sammy seemed to understand what Luke was getting at and took Eoin's hand. "Come on, Eoin. Let's give these two some space, shall we?"

"Why, what's going on?" Anna looked back and forth between her friends.

"Just talk to Luke, honey. We'll be right outside."

Luke reached over the top of the lampshade to test that the bulb was screwed in right. "This doesn't seem like you, Anna," he said, his back to her.

"Oh... um... I just wanted to talk to him about the case."

"What?" Luke turned to look at her. "What are you talking about? I meant the lampshade." He ran a finger along the dangling gold fringe.

Anna laughed out loud. "No, it's not. Can you believe I ordered it online?"

"That doesn't sound like you either." Luke bent down to unplug the lamp from the wall. He lifted the lamp, gently placed it on its side, and unscrewed the base.

"I know. It looked good in the pictures, but as soon as I opened the box, I saw my mistake."

"That's why you should always go to a store to buy something like this in person, right?" Luke's voice was strained as he leaned forward to twist the exposed wires.

"You should have returned it as soon as you saw it wasn't what you wanted."

Anna threw her hands up in frustration. "Will you please stop telling me what I should do!"

"Right." Luke stood. "I need to grab something out of my toolbox. I'll be right back."

Anna perched on the sofa, waiting impatiently. Luke was back within a minute with pliers and a roll of electrical tape.

"So." He got back down to fix the loose wires. "You thought you'd get one thing, but instead you got another. Is that it?"

Anna looked down at her hands. "Are you still talking about the lamp?"

Finishing with the wires, Luke stood the lamp up again and plugged it in. He twisted the switch, and the lamp came on. He shook it just to be sure, but nothing flickered. He finally stopped and turned his full attention to Anna. "You know I talked to Rick. He's not going to sue you."

"You said, thanks. That's good to know."

"I can't do anything about Evan's troubles, though," Luke pointed out. "It's not something Rick can change. Evan's superiors know what happened. He can't make them un-know it."

Heat rose in Anna's cheeks. "That's so unfair."

"Why? Why is it unfair?" Luke shoved his hands in his pockets and turned away from Anna. "Evan told you something he shouldn't have, and now he's paying the price. That sounds perfectly fair to me."

Anna took a step back and felt the sofa against the back of her legs. She stared at Luke as she took a deep breath. "When did we start fighting like this?"

Luke turned back to her and laughed lightly. "When we tried dating. That's why I've been trying to talk to you."

"Why? I don't understand."

"Well, to me, it seems like every time I try to help, it annoys you."

Anna blushed again, this time in shame. "I can see why it seems like that to you. Maybe I'm being oversensitive. I just don't want someone telling me what to do. I want to be independent, to make my own decisions, even to make my own mistakes."

"I never told you what to do."

"You kinda did. From what food to order to how to investigate, you keep giving me directions."

Luke laughed, but it didn't carry the usual joy. "I just wanted to help."

"I know you did, and I appreciate that. So, what does this mean?"

"Friends?" Luke asked, taking her hands in his.

"Friends." Anna nodded. "And I can still call on you for help when I need it, right?"

"I think that's a great idea."

He wrapped her in a hug. She let her head rest on his chest and felt the safety of his strong arms around her as a tear rolled down her cheek.

Sammy and Eoin sat on the porch steps watching passersby making their way up from the beach at the end of a full day or into town for an early dinner. The late-afternoon sun cast long shadows along the lawn and across the street.

Anna plopped down next to them and draped an arm around Eoin. He scooched over to cuddle against her, and she smiled. Bits of conversation floated up from the sidewalk as visitors and residents alike compared notes about last night's storm and what damage they'd seen or experienced.

"How's your luscious Luke?" Sammy asked without looking at her.

"He's fine, but he's not my luscious Luke anymore."

Sammy nodded, still not looking at her. "Are you okay about that?"

Anna thought about it then nodded. "You know, I think I am. It wasn't quite right."

Sammy finally looked at her and grinned. "Yeah, I kinda picked up on that. But you guys are still friends, right?"

"Absolutely." Anna hugged Eoin again. "So, what do we do now? Dinner?"

Eoin nodded enthusiastically, but Sammy shrugged. "Eh. It's a little early, isn't it? Ooh, I know. How about cocktails?"

Anna held up a finger. "I still have leftovers from Corey's visit."

Sammy clambered up. "You stay put. I'll grab them. In the kitchen?"

When Anna nodded, Sammy ran inside. Eoin leaned forward to reach for Tough Cookie, who rolled in the dirt below their feet. The cat toyed with his fingers for a while then sat upright and came closer for a good tickle. Eoin giggled as his fingers played across her fur. The sound of jazz floated out from a passing car. Anna took a deep, relaxing breath and leaned back with her elbows on the step behind her.

"Not bad here, is it?" Sammy came out with three glasses. She handed Eoin the lemonade and Anna one of the Kirs.

"Cheers." Anna held up her glass.

They all clinked glasses, startling Tough Cookie, then sat back, each to their own thoughts.

"So you're not upset?" Sammy asked. "I'm sorry I pushed you to go out with him."

"Don't be," Anna reassured her. "Like you said, the only way to find out if we would get along was to give it a try. Nothing gained, nothing lost, right? Speaking of great ideas, are you willing to share yours yet?"

"Mine?"

Anna nudged Sammy with her shoulder. "You know what I mean. What was that secret plan you put into action? Did it work?"

"Kind of." Sammy made an exaggerated frown before

taking a sip of her Kir. "Except now I have another problem."

Anna raised her eyebrows. "Spill."

"Okay, so I told you someone's been stealing from the bakery, right?"

Anna nodded.

"I knew I couldn't watch everyone all the time—I have four employees, and I'm not always around. But then I realized I have four employees. Right?" She nodded encouragingly at Anna.

"I don't get it," Anna replied.

Sammy sighed. "Unless they're all in on it together, which I seriously doubt, then someone probably saw something. Maybe they didn't realize the other person was stealing. Maybe they just don't want to be a rat. Who knows? But I figured I should take advantage of all my resources."

"That actually makes sense. So what did you do?"

"Hm, don't sound so surprised." Sammy laughed. "I called a staff meeting, got all five of us in a room together, and told them what was happening. I explained that someone had been stealing, at first small things but that they'd moved on to filching cash from the register. They all seemed shocked when I made the announcement, of course."

"I'm guessing the thief did not use the opportunity to jump up and confess?" Anna asked.

"Hardly. But it got everyone's attention."

"All those texts you were getting earlier?"

Sammy nodded. "I was right. Everyone had seen something, but they hadn't had the full picture, hadn't put the pieces together. Once I filled them in, they each let me know what they'd seen."

"And you put it together and know who the culprit is."

"Exactly." Sammy held her glass up, and Anna clinked it with hers.

"Congratulations. That was some good management. What happens now? You said you had another problem."

Sammy nodded. "Now that I know who the thief is, I can fire him. But I don't have any proof. I can't accuse him of stealing."

"You don't need to, though, to let him go."

"I don't, it's true. But if I just let him go, then he'll go somewhere else and keep on stealing from someone else. I feel like I want to do something."

"Why don'tcha call the police?"

Sammy and Anna glanced down. Eoin looked up at them from the flower bed, his knees brown and damp from where he'd been kneeling in the soil to play with Tough Cookie. "If you know someone's a thief, that's what you do, right, Cousin Anna?"

"That's true," Anna agreed. She looked back at Sammy. "Are you thinking of doing that?"

Sammy nodded. "Yep. But I know they won't give me the time of day right now, not with that manhunt still going on."

"Plus, I'm not really sure what they could do. I mean, you can tell them you've been a victim of theft. You can even tell them you have an idea of who's responsible—as long as that person doesn't turn around and file a complaint against you." Anna shuddered.

"Ha! True. Sorry." She leaned over to bump Anna affectionately. "It's not a laughing matter. But that's right, I'm not sure what they can do either. They'll probably tell me to install cameras, and that's expensive. Plus, I can't imagine my thief would be dumb enough to steal on camera."

"Hm, maybe not. But with you and your other

employees watching him now, I bet you'll catch him in the act, come up with some proof."

Sammy nodded. "I hope so. I must have learned something with all the time I spend helping you catch murderers. Maybe I can at least catch a petty thief."

Eoin looked up at them again. "Are you going to catch the murderer again, Cousin Anna?"

Anna stalled, taking another sip of her Kir to buy a few seconds. "I don't know, Eoin. I really don't. I feel like we have so many clues, but I don't see how they fit together."

"Like the oxygen meter," Sammy agreed. "Such an obvious clue, but it could point to either Ralph or Isabelle."

"Exactly."

The number of pedestrians picked up as it passed six o'clock, more and more people heading over to Washington Mall for dinner or drinks. Eoin finished his lemonade and scooted off the porch to play with Tough Cookie in the dirt, dangling a loose flower stem for her to chase.

"Then there's motive," Sammy finally said.

"Or lack thereof," Anna pointed out.

"Dean might have wanted Angela's winery to go out of business."

"Maybe that was what Rick wanted," Anna added.

"Corey might have hated James for the way James dropped him as soon as he got sick."

"Ralph might have wanted to protect his mother, plus he thought he'd benefit as well. As far as he could tell, he couldn't lose."

Sammy laughed. "So basically, we can come up with reasons for why everyone might want to kill James Longhurst. What a guy."

Eoin dropped the plant and skipped back up the porch steps. "Is it dinnertime yet?" He asked brightly.

"Always hungry, aren't you?" Anna asked. "Sure, we can go in."

"Wait, before you eat." Sammy stood, brushing off her jeans. "You mentioned you might like to play soccer, right, Eoin?"

The boy nodded, his red curls bouncing.

"Come on, then. I saw a sign saying the men's soccer team had practice right about now. Let's go watch." Sammy put out a hand, and Eoin grabbed it eagerly.

The three of them traipsed off the porch and up the street in the direction of the municipal playing fields. Only a few puddles remained on the shadiest patches of sidewalk, the sun having dried up everything else. Lawns told a different story, though, as Anna spied patches of mud running along the sidewalk and crisscrossing previously neat front yards. She kept a close eye out for mud patches as they walked, pulling Eoin away from any potential messes.

The playing field was in no better condition. If Anna didn't know better, she would think a herd of cattle had stampeded through it. Though one look at the players made it obvious that they were the ones who'd been rolling around in the mud. They must have been playing for a while, given the condition of the men and the pitch. Eoin let out a hoot and ran along the sidelines, following the ball, waving and calling to whoever had control of it at the time.

Anna wasn't sure if the men appreciated Eoin's attempts to coach them, but no one complained, so she let him continue, though she might have to drop him fully clothed into the bathtub when they got home.

As she watched, she recognized Evan as one of the muddier players on the field. Streaks of brown ran up and down his legs, gathering in the clefts of his calf muscles and running up his thighs. She'd never thought about his thighs before. Apparently his uniform hid some well-developed muscles. Sammy seemed to enjoy the view, too, as she shifted her stance occasionally, bending her head this way and that.

"See something you like?" Anna teased her.

Sammy showed no embarrassment. "Absolutely. Don't you?"

Anna laughed and returned her attention to Eoin, whose enthusiasm caused him to take a couple of tumbles in the slippery mud. Each time, he popped back up before she could react. She felt the weight of responsibility for him more than she had before, probably because his visit was becoming a little more permanent. She would be his legal guardian, at least temporarily. That was a big deal, but she was ready for it.

Sammy caught the direction of her gaze. "We're standing next to a field of big, muscular men, and you're watching Eoin. I love it."

Anna laughed again. "I love him. I really do. You know I would do anything to protect him."

"I know, honey. You'll be great at it. It must be an amazing thing, to be a mother, to be responsible for a little person. I guess even women like Isabelle must feel that way about their sons."

Anna raised an eyebrow. "Hmm. I find that hard to believe."

"Oh, I don't know. She's still his mother. And you said Corey said they loved each other."

Anna chewed on her lip, her eyes following the soccer players as they chased one another back to the far goal but her mind going over everything Corey had told her about the Longhursts. "From what Corey said, the relationships in that family were pretty strange."

"James and Isabelle intentionally annoying each other, you mean?"

"That's part of it. They were competing against each other, too, weren't they?"

"Ha! To see who could annoy the other the most, you mean?"

Anna laughed. "Well, yes, but not just that. They were competing over Ralph."

"I thought Corey said it wasn't really a fair competition, that Ralph liked his mother more."

Anna looked at her friend, her eyes open wide. "Of course, that's it!"

Sammy took a step back, startled. "What's it?"

"I think I finally understand the motive." Anna grinned.

Sammy opened her mouth to speak, but a whistle sounded, and the men trotted off the field.

$\text{\textbf{\&\quad 42\quad \&}}$

Eoin ran to meet Evan as he jogged to his gym bag lying on the bleachers. He grabbed Evan's hand and led him back to Anna and Sammy. Anna tried unsuccessfully not to picture falling into Evan's arms at the winery. Evan may have been dealing with a similar struggle, as he smiled uncomfortably at Anna and looked quickly away.

"Evan, I'm sorry I keep bugging you. I didn't know you'd be here."

Evan offered a half smile. "It's okay. What do you need?"

"We came to watch the practice," Sammy explained. "Our little man here is interested in soccer."

"I am." Eoin bobbed his head. "I can kick the ball really hard." He swung his leg out to kick at an imaginary ball, almost losing his balance in the process.

Anna put a firm hand on his shoulder before he toppled over again. "Since you're here, Evan, I have been thinking about the case. I think I have an idea."

Evan sighed. "Anna, I do want to talk to you but not

about the case. I've been told to stay away from you. I got an official reprimand for what I did."

"I'm so sorry about that. I really am. But this is serious. I need to tell you what we found."

A sharp buzz from Evan's bag cut off whatever reply he might have given her. Pulling his phone out of the bag, he saw the caller ID and clicked to answer. "Sir."

Anna and Sammy exchanged glances. "More trouble?" Anna mouthed the words to Sammy.

Sammy shook her head as she shrugged then opened her eyes wide in a crazy-person look.

Anna laughed then slapped her hand over her mouth as Evan glared at her and put his hand over his other ear. He only said a few more words into the phone before hanging up.

He turned back to the women, a broad smile on his face. "Great news. They caught the killer."

"The killer? I thought you arrested Isabelle," Anna said, confused.

Evan lowered his brows for a moment, then his face cleared, and he laughed. "No, not the person who killed James Longhurst. The shooter from Trenton, the one we've been looking for."

"That is great news," Sammy agreed. "Finally."

"Okay, okay, give us a break. It took a few days, but we got our man, right?"

"How'd they do it?" Anna asked. "How'd they finally find him?"

Evan let out a small laugh. "Really good luck, I'm afraid —well, bad luck for him, stupid luck, actually."

"Meaning...?" Sammy prompted him.

"The guy was staying with friends in Wildwood. Last night's storm took out their power, including their air conditioning. When it got too hot inside the house, the suspect decided to sit outside on the back deck for a while."

"Wait, he's in hiding from the police and decided to get a little tan?" Anna asked in amazement.

"Hey, no one ever said criminals were smart. In fact, it's usually the opposite. A police helicopter spotted him, and that was that. He didn't even try to run."

"At least jail has air conditioning." Sammy laughed then stopped. "It does, right?"

"Not our concern," Evan answered. "Wow, what a relief."

He pulled a towel out of his gym bag and started wiping some of the mud off his arms and legs. When his glance fell on Eoin, he pulled the boy over and started wiping him down too. Eoin wriggled a bit but let Evan do his best.

"You know, it was Eoin who figured out our latest clue." Anna smiled at the sight of Evan trying to clean Eoin.

"Oh yeah?" Evan asked Eoin. "What did you work out?"

Anna pulled up the pictures of the oxygen meter. "He recognized what these scratches must mean." Anna pointed at the scratches so Evan could see what she was talking about. "This is from when the killer tried to make the meter work the way he wanted it to."

"Make it not work," Sammy clarified.

"I figured it out," Eoin agreed, beaming.

"Whoa, hold up." Evan held up his hands. "The killer put the faulty meter back in the winery. So what's the connection with this one?"

"Practice," Sammy said confidently, smiling at Eoin. "Look how messed up it is. He wasn't sure how to make it do what he needed, so he tried a few different approaches. Looks like he tried to pry it open and tamper with the mechanics."

"But I guess that didn't work. Plus, it turns out there

was a much easier way to do it, anyway, by simply calibrating it incorrectly," Anna said.

Evan frowned. "Interesting."

Eoin jumped in. "It makes sense, y'know. If I need to figure something out, and I don't know how to do it, I keep trying different ways until I get it."

"So whoever did this is not someone who uses these meters often. They're not something the person knows intimately," Evan pointed out.

"That's true."

"And that points at Isabelle. Is that your idea? That this proves Isabelle killed her husband?"

Anna shook her head, but Sammy raised a hand. "I know you don't like it, Anna, but she was in the office. She could have left it there."

"I just don't think that's it. I think I know exactly who left it there and why they killed James—and it's not Isabelle. You've arrested the wrong person." Anna's frustration rose.

"I'm impressed you found this, Anna, and even figured out what these scratches might mean," Evan said kindly. "But it's not enough. Why shouldn't Ralph happen to have the same kind of oxygen meter? It doesn't prove that this is related to the death at Angela's winery."

"Why would Ralph have an oxygen meter at all?" Anna paced in front of Evan, thinking furiously. "He doesn't need them for his work."

"Maybe it was his dad's, and he left it in the office."

"Phht." Anna rolled her eyes as she let out a frustrated breath. "Why would James be tampering with an oxygen meter?"

Sammy and Evan exchanged glances as Anna kept pacing. "It makes sense... it's a good reason... he wouldn't expect what happened..." Anna stopped pacing and ran her hand over her face in exhaustion. "I know who tampered with this and why, but we don't have enough evidence. Luke was right after all. I should have been focusing more on hard evidence."

Sammy put an arm around her friend. "Stop being so tough on yourself. You do have real evidence, just not quite enough. Kind of like me at the bakery, right?"

Anna put her hands on her hips and turned away from the field. Her gaze ran to the line of gingerbread houses across Lafayette Street, each of them lovingly maintained by people who worked hard to keep them up, to keep Cape May picturesque. That was what she loved about this town, the way everyone put the work in to keep the history alive, to keep the town beautiful. This was a close and caring community. How could a killer possibly get away with murder here?

Her eyes widened, and she smiled, turning back to her friends. "Sammy, you're a genius."

"I am?"

Anna nodded. "We need to have a little party."

$\mathfrak{R}$ 43 $\mathfrak{R}$

"I don't know how I let you convince me this was a good idea. I'm clearly too tired to think straight," Detective Walsh grumbled, rubbing his eyes as he leaned against Evan's desk.

A handful of officers moved through the room, sorting mail, checking email, taking stock of what they needed to get back to after having been so focused on the manhunt for the past few days. Despite the relative crowd—compared to the last time Anna was there—the room was hushed. Officers moved silently, and when they spoke, it was in low tones.

"It wasn't me, sir. It was the evidence," Evan replied. "You saw the meter. You know what it must mean."

"I know what it *might* mean, and I know it's not enough to release Isabelle." Detective Walsh looked at Anna. "Just because I've been working my tail off helping the Trenton PD with their manhunt doesn't mean I haven't been paying attention to this case. I know the facts."

"Anna thinks—" Evan started then cut himself off. "That is, I'm sure this is the only way to get the truth."

Walsh pushed himself off the desk. "Well, it seems you have proved useful in the past, Ms. McGregor. It's probably the exhaustion speaking, but I'm willing to go along with this tonight." Walsh looked them each in the eye. "But when this is over, we are going to have a conversation about when it is and when it isn't appropriate to rely on information from the public."

"Understood," Evan said just as Rick Enright's voice carried from the station entrance.

Evan stood to greet him while Anna spun on her heel and slipped out of the room before Rick could see her. Pausing just beyond the door, she held her breath and listened. If Rick didn't agree to the plan, the whole thing could fall apart. She needed everyone there.

"Thank you for coming down, Mr. Enright," Walsh said. "I know it's late. We won't take up more of your time than necessary."

"Why am I here?" Rick's voice sounded rough and angry. "Is this an apology?"

"Of sorts. I'm sorry to ask you this, but would you mind waiting for just a few minutes? I'll tell you what, you can wait in the main building. You'll be more comfortable there."

Anna jogged down the hall and turned into the auditorium ahead of Evan, who escorted Rick the same way. Used for everything from town award ceremonies to holiday concerts, the municipal building's auditorium had a stage at one end with folding metal chairs scattered somewhat randomly around the room.

Anna skipped up the stairs onto the stage, where she joined Sammy and Eoin behind the curtain. Peeking out, she saw Evan guiding Rick into the room.

Rick stopped when he saw who else was already there.

"Is this some kind of joke? I don't need to be here, you know."

"It's no joke, Mr. Enright. I assure you, you'll want to be here," Evan replied.

Rick took a step back, but Evan stood firm, a pleasant but neutral expression on his face. Rick finally shoved his hands into his jacket pockets and moved to a chair on the far side of the room, well away from where Ralph and Corey already sat. No more than a minute later, Detective Walsh came in with Dean and Angela.

"Angela? What's going on?" Rick jumped up.

Angela hurried over to him, placing a hand on his arm. "I don't know. Anna asked me to come. She said this would answer all our questions."

"Anna?" He looked around. "So where is she? I've got some things to say to her."

"Shh." Angela glanced around. Everyone else was staring at them. "Just sit down, okay? I don't know what's going on, but there's only one way to find out, right?"

Rick grumbled but sat as Angela perched on a chair next to him.

"Well, who does know what we're doing here?" Dean asked, looking at Corey. "Who invited you?"

"He did." Corey pointed at Evan. "Called and asked me to come down for questioning." Corey looked questioningly at Ralph, but Ralph remained silent.

"That sounds ominous." Dean grabbed a chair near the stage and leaned forward with his forearms on his legs, peering at Evan. "Okay, we're here. What's going on?"

Detective Walsh moved to the front of the room near the stage and cleared his throat. "Ladies and gentlemen, thank you again for coming down tonight on such short notice. I know I owe you all an explanation. It's a little complicated, I'm afraid."

He glanced back at the curtain behind him, and Anna recognized her cue. Leaving Sammy waiting behind the curtain with Eoin, Anna stepped out onto the stage then jumped down next to Detective Walsh.

Rick's chair squeaked across the floor as he stood in a rush. "What is this? What's going on?"

"It's okay. I told you Anna invited me." Angela stood, too, once again putting a hand on Rick's arm. "I figured she'd be here. Come on, sit down."

Angela murmured a few more calming words, and eventually, Rick resumed his seat. But if the color in his cheeks was any indication, he was neither calm nor happy to be there.

"We're here to find the truth about what happened to James Longhurst," Anna started.

Rick jumped up again. "The truth about James Longhurst? Don't you already have the killer in jail?" Rick turned on Walsh. "I don't get this at all."

"We do have a suspect in custody, that's true," Walsh acknowledged. "But we're still short a few details. I thought you'd want to be here to hear this, given your..." He glanced at Evan. "Well, given your bad experience with this investigation."

"Of course I want to hear the truth. I just don't see why we should listen to her." He pointed at Anna.

"Because I asked her to help, remember?" Angela's voice sounded strained. "Rick, just sit down, will you?"

"Do you know she thought I did it? She thought I killed James." Rick sat and took both of Angela's hands in his. "As if I could ever do anything that would hurt you."

"I know, Rick. I believe you." Angela smiled, tightening her grip around his. They each leaned slightly closer in their chairs, their heads almost touching.

Detective Walsh rubbed his hands together and turned to Anna. "Right, then. Let's get on with this."

44

"Detective Walsh brought you all here tonight because the wrong person has been arrested for the murder of James Longhurst." Anna moved around the room as she spoke.

Corey shifted in his chair to follow her with her eyes. "If the police know they have the wrong person, why is she still in jail?"

"Good question." Anna made her way closer to him and Ralph. "That's why we're here—to expose the truth and the real killer."

Dean's chair creaked as he resettled himself onto it. "Are you suggesting one of us is the killer?"

Before Anna could answer, Evan held up a clear plastic bag, the bright-yellow oxygen meter clearly visible within. "Angela, do you recognize this?"

Angela looked at it from where she sat without getting up. "Sure, it's the same kind of meter I use in the winery."

Evan looked at Ralph. "We found this in Ralph's office when we arrested his mother."

"Well… but… why shouldn't I have an oxygen meter?" Ralph spoke for the first time that evening.

"You don't need that for your work, Ralph." Corey's brows furrowed. "Why would you have that?"

"Is it yours, Ralph?" Anna asked.

"Yes, it's mine. I'm in the wine business." Ralph spoke slowly, sitting up straighter as he talked. "I like to learn about the tools of the trade—what they are, how they work. Even though I don't need an oxygen meter now, you never know when that knowledge will come in handy while I'm working on developing new contacts, new clients."

"That makes sense, I guess," Dean said doubtfully, his expression reflecting his hesitancy rather than supporting his words. "I don't have those kinds of conversations with my distributor, but hey, why not?"

"Which is why I've been telling you that you need a new distributor." Ralph smiled at him. "You know I'm available."

"Are you trying to land a deal while your mother is sitting in jail for a crime she may not have committed?" Corey's eyes widened.

"Sorry," Ralph mumbled, looking down at his hands.

"Come to think of it, I never asked you." Dean stood and walked over to Ralph. "Why did you tell Anna that you were with me the day your dad died? You know you weren't."

"I just thought…" Ralph looked around, his gaze falling on Walsh and Evan. "I didn't want her to suspect you."

"That's very thoughtful of you, but I have plenty of staff who will tell you I was in the winery all day, from early in the morning, without taking a break."

Anna spoke up. "That's not true, Dean. You were seen in town, meeting with Anthony Middleton."

Dean spun around to glare at Anna. "What? Were you following me or something?" He took a few steps closer to her. "And why shouldn't I meet with him?"

Ralph smirked. "If it was so innocent, then why are you lying about where you were?"

Dean huffed and shook his head. "I do not need to discuss my business plans with the general public." He glared at Anna again. "If you know I met with Anthony, then I assume you know what it was about?"

"If you met with Anthony, then I probably know what it was about." Corey twisted in his seat to look at Dean. "And I admit, I'm surprised."

"Care to illuminate the rest of us?" Walsh asked. "Dean? Corey?"

Dean just shrugged and returned to his seat. "Anthony is looking for someone to buy ten acres out towards Higbee Beach."

"You're buying more land? Why is that so secret?" Anna asked.

Corey grinned. "It's gravelly, loamy soil. Ideal terroir for Bordeaux grapes, I understand."

"It's true, so what?" Dean sat up straight and looked boldly around the room. "Yeah, I'm going to plant some French varietals. It will be a few years before they're worth trying, but I figured I'd give it a shot."

"You? Why?" Ralph asked.

"Why not?" Dean seemed genuinely surprised by the question. "I'm always looking for ways to grow and improve my business."

"Oh, well, I just thought... um... you know, your commitment to traditional New Jersey grapes."

"Well, whatever you thought, you thought wrong."

Ralph blinked for a second then stood and turned to

Evan. "Look, what is this all about? Can I have my meter back now? I'm not sure you even had permission to take it out of my office."

Anna watched everything closely, thinking. "Angela, can you take a closer look at the meter? See how it's been scratched and recalibrated?"

Evan handed it to her as Anna stood next to Angela, ignoring Rick's glares and Ralph's sputters.

"I already told you, I like to learn about the tools of the trade. Why shouldn't I mess around with my property?" Ralph asked.

Angela turned the meter over in her hands then laughed. "What do you know? It's my meter."

"How can you tell?" Anna asked.

"That." Angela pointed. A small sticker, almost invisible against the black back of the meter, held a QR code. "I put these on all my property to keep track of them. Oh, well, that was the plan anyway." She blushed. "I didn't even realize this was missing."

"This is definitely your meter?" Evan asked.

"It's got to be. You can check the QR code. It'll take you to my property register."

The room fell silent as everyone grappled with what this might mean. A loud crack broke the silence as Dean snapped his fingers. "Of course, you mentioned that Angela didn't have a lot of visitors that day."

"What are you talking about? What day?"

Dean's eyes narrowed as he stood. "The day your father died."

"I never said that," Ralph spluttered, reaching behind him as he slid back onto his chair.

"Yeah, you did. We were talking, and you let that slip. Then you immediately took it back, said you were there over the weekend. I didn't think anything of it. But you were there on Monday. You were at White Pines Winery the day James was killed."

Corey jumped up and turned on Ralph. "You asked me about those meters. Just casual conversation, I thought. Where you could get one, which ones were the best, and why? But that was all part of your plan. You messed with Angela's oxygen meter, recalibrated it so it wouldn't work correctly." He backed away from Ralph.

Rick stood as well, but he moved closer to Ralph.

"You cut the ventilation line in Angela's winery, too, didn't you? You could have killed her."

Walsh put a hand on Rick's arm to stop his forward progress. Rick took a step back.

"You have no proof of that," Ralph said, but his voice shook.

"I'll swear in a court of law you told me you were there that day," Dean said.

"And I'll bear witness to your interest in those meters." Corey's whole body shook. "You would let your mother take the blame for a murder you committed? I can't believe I was your friend. I thought you were... human."

Ralph jumped up, his hands balled into fists at his sides. "Human? You want to talk about human? How about the way my father treated my mother and me? Goading, teasing, ridiculing." His voice rose as his face turned bright red. "He treated us like dirt, not like humans. Not like family. I just wanted... I thought my mother..." He slumped back into his chair, his energy drained. His head tipped forward, his chin down to his chest. "Enough of this. I want a lawyer."

"Sure thing. You can make that call from my office." Detective Walsh put a hand on Ralph's arm. "I have a few more questions for you, once your lawyer gets here, of course." Walsh nodded at Evan.

They escorted Ralph out of the room.

❧ 45 ☙

Anna took her time, answering the many questions from the people gathered there. Sammy and Eoin joined her, providing their versions of the events of the past few days, what they had learned, and how.

An hour later, they left the town hall through the front door, walking through the darkened front garden that Anna had sat in only the day before. So much had happened since then. It seemed more like a week than a day. They followed the path down to the street, where a large black BMW waited for them. As they approached, the back window rolled down.

"I understand I have you to thank for my freedom," Isabelle said through the half-open window, her perfectly made-up face just visible in the glow from the car's overhead light.

Anna leaned down to look in the window. Eoin stood on his toes to try seeing in then gave up and turned back to the front yard.

"I'm sorry you had to go through all this. It can't have been easy for you," Anna said.

"I lost my husband. It's true. But to tell the truth, I lost him years ago. Our marriage was a convenience only."

"And your son?" Sammy asked.

"That will take some getting used to." Isabelle dabbed a tear from her eye, gently avoiding her eyeliner. "I never thought he could do something like that."

Anna nodded. "You aren't as much of a pushover as he expected."

"Oh, I let James have his way. It was easier. But with him gone, that part of me is gone too. I'm in control now. I won't let anyone treat me like that again." The gravel in Isabelle's voice left no doubt about her strength.

"Something Corey told me made me think about Ralph, and it might be meaningful for you. Ralph may have rationalized killing James at least in part based on the way James treated you. Ralph loves you in his own way. He thought he'd be helping you by killing James."

"He loves me so much he was willing to let me rot in jail," Isabelle scoffed.

"There's that," Sammy agreed.

"But thank you. Really, thank you. I don't know if the police would have figured that out. I could still be in jail if it weren't for you," Isabelle said with feeling.

"I like to think they would have," Anna said, speaking up for her friends on the force.

"You would. You're their friend. I have my doubts. Thank God for a good lawyer on speed dial," Isabelle said. "You have a talent for digging up the truth, Anna. I'm glad you're putting it to good use."

Anna stood and watched as the BMW pulled silently away and glided down the road.

"Anna!"

Evan came jogging down the path.

Sammy took Eoin's hand. "I need to get this kid back home and to bed, don't I?" She winked at Anna.

Anna wasn't sure what Sammy was winking about, but she turned and joined Evan to stroll along the sidewalk toward Washington Mall. It was a beautiful Saturday night, and more people seemed to be out and about after the big storm. Crowds of visitors moved up and down the pedestrianized street as small white lights twinkled in the trees overhead.

"Evan, I am so sorry," Anna said.

"For what?" Evan asked, surprised.

"For what? For getting you into trouble. For egging you on to do something you shouldn't have done. I think of myself as the kind of person who's always there for her friends, and instead of helping you, I really let you down. I can't forgive myself for that."

"What are you talking about? You didn't do that, Anna. I made my own choices. I always do." He nudged her. "Just like you do."

"Hm," Anna huffed out a disbelieving breath. "I still feel really bad. I hope I can make it up to you."

"I keep telling you, there's nothing to make up. We make our choices, and we deal with the consequences. Speaking of which, have you decided to go back to finish your PhD?"

Anna looked up at him in surprise. "How did you know that was what I was going to decide?"

Evan winked and grinned at her. "I guess I know you too well. Um." He paused then cleared his throat. "I also know that you and Luke aren't seeing each other anymore."

"News travels fast. Yes, that's true."

"Are you okay with it?"

Anna shrugged. "We agreed to stay friends. I guess he's

looking for something different. He reminds me of Rick in that way."

"You need a boyfriend who respects you for who you are, not who he thinks you are or who he wants you to be. Someone who respects your choices."

"Very profound. Do you have someone in mind?"

Evan laughed. "Anna, you must know what I'm thinking."

She stopped and looked at him, shaking her head. "I never seem to know what you're thinking."

Evan took both her hands in his. "How could you not know how I feel about you?"

Anna blinked. "How you feel about me? But I'm always getting in your way." She grimaced and looked down. "Even getting you into trouble. You'd be better off if I kept my distance."

"Anna." He took her face in both his hands. "You could never be in the way." And then he kissed her.

CURIOUS ABOUT THE COCKTAIL?

The Kir is a simple cocktail of complicated origins. Crème de cassis, a black currant liqueur, was popular in late-nineteenth-century France. A specialty of the Burgundy region of France, it became common in cafes around the country, as patrons would add a drop to a variety of beverages. The story is that after World War II, Felix Kir, a mayor in Burgundy, got in the habit of offering a particularly good mix to visiting dignitaries: crème de cassis and a local white wine. The drink has been named the Kir in his honor.

But why did Felix Kir promote this new drink? Was it a creative marketing tool for local produce or a clever way to hide inferior wine? Crème de cassis is produced in Burgundy, and a Kir is traditionally served with a white Burgundy wine, so by popularizing this cocktail, Mayor Kir successfully drove up interest in two significant local businesses. Another factor to consider, however, is that during the war, the German army confiscated all of Burgundy's red wine. That left towns in Burgundy with only their white wine—a wine not well known and perhaps not much admired. Mayor Kir's solution solved the excess wine problem by adding a new and interesting twist. So did he do it to promote local products or to make the best of a bad wine? I suspect there is truth to both interpretations. A creative mixologist solved a problem with a clever business tactic, and we've all benefitted!

The classic Kir is made with crème de cassis. However, when I ordered a Kir in France a few years ago, the waiter asked how I wanted it made: with crème de cassis (blackcurrant), de mûre (blackberry), de pêche (peach), or framboise (raspberry). I tried it with peach, and it was wonderful!

Traditionally made with a dry white Burgundy wine, a Kir works well with any dry white wine. It also works fabulously with champagne. When made with champagne, it's called a Kir Royale. I have a particular fondness for Kir Royales, since they were the signature cocktail my husband and I chose for our Cape May wedding!

Ingredients

    4 oz dry white wine (Sauvignon Blanc works well)
    1 oz crème de cassis

Pour the crème de cassis into a wine glass and add the white wine. Adjust quantities to taste and enjoy!

CAPE MAY WINERIES

Cape May has a number of great wineries, and to the best of my knowledge, no one has ever died in one! Wine growers have been producing wine in New Jersey before the land was called New Jersey. Two New Jersey residents, William Alexander and Edward Antill, took up a challenge in 1758 from Great Britain's Royal Society to produce a colonial wine. Their efforts won them two hundred pounds from the Royal Society, and the New Jersey wine trade was born.

While the wine industry in New Jersey continued to grow in the nineteenth and twentieth centuries, it has seen exponential growth in the new millennium. Despite its reputation for producing sweet wines, more and more vintners in New Jersey are experimenting with different blends, different varietals, that can stand up against many California wines. And they're getting better every year. There are four designated American Viticultural Areas in the state: Warren Hills AVA, Central Delaware Valley AVA, the Outer Coastal Plain AVA, and of course, Cape May Peninsula. For a region to be approved by the federal government as an AVA, it must be able to prove that it is a good area for grape growing. Criteria used to evaluate regions include climate, soil type, and other features—including the history of wine grape growing.

New Jersey vineyards produce a number of grapes. Growing conditions vary throughout the state, which means that each region produces noticeably different wines. In general, the most common white varietals grown in the state are Albarino, Chardonnay, Gruner Veltliner, Petit Manseng and Riesling. Leading red varietals include Cabernet Franc, Cabernet Sauvignon, Pinot Noir, and Merlot. And then there are the French-American hybrids that seem to flourish in New Jersey, including Chambourcin, Vidal Blanc, and Vignoles.

So what's grown in Cape May? The Cape May Peninsula is a sub-area of the 2.25 million acres of the Outer Coastal Plain AVA. The Cape May Peninsula is bordered entirely by water and the Pinelands National Reserve. It has the most frost-free days in the state and offers the longest growing season for grapes in the state. This part of New Jersey tends to be flatter, with well-drained, loamy sand soils that have lots of gravel. With this terroir, red and white Bordeaux varieties do very well.

Have you tried a New Jersey wine? If so, have you tried one recently?

A NOTE FROM THE AUTHOR

Anna's story isn't over yet! Stay tuned for the next book in the series, coming next year. To stay on top of what's coming, follow me on social media (the links are provided at the end of this note) or sign up for my newsletter. You can find my newsletter signup on my website at janegorman.com.

I hope you enjoyed reading this latest saga in Anna's story. If you loved it - and even if you just liked it! - please consider leaving a review. I can't stress enough how valuable these reviews are for authors and book sellers.

While I usually write alone, I have so many people to thank for their help in creating this fictional version of Cape May. Thank you to my creative and collegial support team from Table 25: James McCrone, Jane Kelly, Matty Dalrymple and Lisa Regan. I could not write without you all! Thank you also to all the members of Sisters in Crime, from the Delaware Valley Chapter and the Guppies, for invaluable support with writing, marketing, and generally staying sane during the publication process.

Cape May is, of course, a real town. But the version of Cape May that appears in the Cape May Cozy Mysteries with a Twist is quite fictionalized. While I use several real places, I add fictional touches where necessary and occasionally I create new places out of whole cloth, including White Pine

Winery. I do recommend visiting Cape May. It's true, there's something for everyone in this fabulous, historic beach town!

Jane Gorman

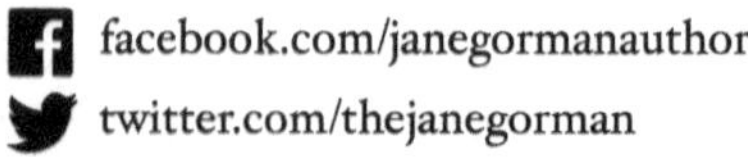

ALSO BY JANE GORMAN

Cape May Cozy Mysteries With a Twist

Scones and Scofflaws

Boats, Bodies, and the Bee's Knees

Killers and Kir Royale

The Adam Kaminski Mystery Series

A Blind Eye

A Thin Veil

All That Glitters

What She Fears

A Pale Reflection

The Bitter Truth

www.ingramcontent.com/pod-product-compliance
Lightning Source LLC
Chambersburg PA
CBHW021650110726
47902CB00007B/1901